SAVAGE
ISLE

SAVAGE ISLE

Beautiful Isolated Deadly

BEVERLEY SCHERBERGER

Copyright © 2017 by Beverley Scherberger
Second Edition Copyright © 2021 by Beverley Scherberger

ISBN-13: 978-1981493845
ISBN-10: 1981493840

Imprint: Independently published

All rights reserved. No part of this publication may be reproduced, distributed, or transmitted in any form or by any means including photocopying, recording, or other electronic or mechanical methods without the express written permission of the publisher except for the use of brief quotations in a critical book review.

This is a work of fiction. Names, characters, and incidents are a product of the author's imagination. Locales and public names are sometimes used for atmospheric purposes. Any resemblance to actual people, living or dead, or to businesses, companies, or events is entirely coincidental.

Printed in the United States of America

OTHER TITLES BY BEVERLEY SCHERBERGER

STRANDED

Saving Serena

Legacy of the Fallen Angel

INSATIABLE: Book #1 of the Alien Hunger Series

The Problem with Men

For those who wanted more of the story.

ACKNOWLEDGMENTS

This book would not have been written except for the many readers of *STRANDED* who fell in love with the characters, felt the hair on the backs of their necks stand up, and wanted more. What an incredible compliment! But instead of creating Book 2, I decided to go back and give you the *what-happened-before* part of the tale. Thank you for your requests.

I owe a special debt of gratitude to Carol Buhler who took off the gloves and bluntly told me what she liked and what she didn't. Her expertise and insight forced me to make changes I would otherwise have overlooked. I appreciate you more than you know. Thanks, Carol.

Thank you, also, to the Cotacachi Writers Group who supported, encouraged, and motivated me. Your comments and suggestions have made the story better, more real, and forced me to provide the excitement and emotion my readers asked for. This second edition contains two additional chapters that the original version did not.

All authors yearn for a graphic designer who understands them and can take a vision for a book jacket, improve on it, and make it better than we could ever have dreamed, knowing that a book is, indeed, judged by its cover. I've found such a gem. Thanks, Janet Dado—you're the greatest!

If I've missed anyone, please know that it's not on purpose and that you've been thanked many times over in my heart.

PART I

Chapter 1

"LOOK OUT!"

Fierce screeching and snarling nearly drowned out the high-pitched human screams. Too late, I saw the vicious monkey reach through the bars to grab Artie's arm, my wasted warning hanging in the air as razor-sharp fangs sank deeply into the man's flesh. Two other monkeys darted to the aid of their cellmate and the three yanked their prey face-first against the cage as though trying to squeeze him completely through the metal rails. I had no doubt that was their intent.

An agonized scream fueled my sprint around the maze of tables and countertop workspaces as arterial blood painted the ceiling a deep red. Artie fell to the floor, minus his right arm.

Angry chatter, snarls, and growls accompanied the grisly wet gnawing as the animals feasted on the stolen limb.

I dragged my friend's inert form out of the beasts' reach and heard a low moan. *My God, he's still alive!* Deep bites on the right side of his face exposed white bone—clear evidence the animals had tried to tear out his throat. Only the narrow-spaced bars had protected the jugular.

Keying the walkie-talkie on my belt with one hand, I tried to stem the bleeding with the other. The spurts from the torn shoulder slowed, the diminishing crimson arc a clear indication Artie was losing the battle.

"I need medics in Building Two asap!" I yelled frantically. "Artie's lost an arm."

Although I applied pressure with both hands on the destroyed socket, blood streamed through my fingers.

Almost immediately, the double doors burst open. My husband Carl and two white-coated doctors dashed to my side just as the flow slackened to a dribble. I knew, even before Dr. Chen spoke, that Artie was gone.

"There's no pulse. I'm sorry."

He pronounced time of death and the doctors stepped away from the body, so Carl could help me to my feet.

"Are you okay?" he asked, holding me at arms' length and looking me over. Worry etched deep furrows in his forehead.

I nodded.

He frowned and shook his head. "What happened? How'd they get hold of him?"

"I don't know. I was over there…" I pointed across the room. "…when I heard an odd sound and glanced back just as Jock grabbed Artie's sleeve. You know how incredibly strong they are. He tried to pull free but the other two monkeys jumped in and he didn't stand a chance against the three."

Hanging my head, I replayed the gruesome scene in my mind. "Before I could get to the pen, they'd ripped his arm off." I trembled and sobbed. "There was so much blood… I couldn't make it stop."

Oblivious to the red smears my hands made on his white coat and with anger in his voice, Carl pulled me close and pressed his chin to the top of my head. He growled against my hair, "What was he doing so close to the cage? Dammit, he *knew* better!"

We had worked with Artie for three years. He was a dependable, conscientious worker. But with these beasts, a lack of concentration for only one second could prove catastrophic.

Dr. Chen radioed for a gurney while Carl took my hand and led me to our quarters—away from the grisly scene. Losing a friend and co-worker under such horrible circumstances had drained my energy and any enthusiasm I'd felt for the afternoon's work. After I washed away the blood and changed my clothes, we stretched out on the bed and he held me until I quit shaking.

An hour later I awoke, surprised that I'd been able to fall asleep. Feeling more in control of my emotions I rose, fixed a cup of tea, and joined Carl in the living room.

He looked up, his bushy brows forming a question. "Are you okay?" he asked softly. "Feeling better?"

"Yes. Not so shaky," I replied, his apparent concern touching my heart. *What would I do without him?*

We sat in companionable silence for a few minutes, then, taking a deep breath, I said, "I've been thinking..."

He sighed, set aside his book, and uncrossed his long, gangly legs. I knew he hated it when I prefaced a conversation with that phrase. Inevitably, we ended up at odds with each other.

"What is it now, Laralee?"

"We need more space. I'm afraid more people will die like Artie did. What if we ask the Spanish government to consider erecting additional buildings or, maybe moving the experiments to a different location?"

I could see him pondering my suggestion, various emotions flitting across his craggy features. His brown mop of unruly hair needed a trim and the stubble on his square jaw seemed especially pronounced. His dark eyes settled on mine.

"I don't know. There isn't enough suitable land on this tiny island to build another large-animal enclosure. I suppose we could ask about a new location."

He seemed to be considering it, so I added, "If they want the experiments to continue without further loss of life, *something* has to be done. The serum has boosted the monkeys' intelligence as well as their appetite. I feel like they're watching us, learning our moves, and figuring out how to defeat us. Are we experimenting on them or vice versa? We need more safeguards."

"Yes, I agree," he nodded. "Last month when King Louie escaped and let those other monkeys out, we nearly had a mutiny on our hands. We were lucky to put them down before they got to you."

I shuddered at the memory, stood, and went to the kitchen to refill my tea. Raising my voice to be heard from the other room, I said, "And in addition to the safety issue, it put us behind in the experiments because the four animals we killed were the most advanced. Losing people is unacceptable. Losing monkeys is a loss to the program and we just don't have the space here to perform safely at maximum capability."

Returning, I took my seat. "Surely, the Spanish would understand that."

He nodded and gazed into my eyes. "I don't know what I'd do if something happened to you and I hadn't done everything I could to keep you safe." He rose and changed seats, sitting next to me on the couch. Draping one arm around my shoulder, he nuzzled my neck. "My heart nearly stopped this morning when I heard your frantic voice on the radio. I'll draft a letter to the Spanish Committee on Scientific Experiments tonight."

Chapter 2

THE NEXT MORNING, I rose early. Gruesome nightmares had filled my sleep and I woke exhausted. However, it was Orangutan Thursday—my favorite day of the week—and I perked up at the thought of working with my favorite student.

As I dressed, I recalled my husband's diligence at his desk the previous evening. "Carl, did you finish that letter last night?" He had still been working on it when I went to bed.

"Yes, finally," he answered from the kitchen table. "I wanted it worded 'just so' for maximum impact. I'll send it via the supply ship that should come next week. Who knows when we'll get an answer, though." He sipped his coffee. "You seem pretty chipper this morning after such a restless night."

"Did I keep you up?"

"A little. You tossed and turned and moaned in your sleep. Not surprising after the incident with Artie. Are you okay this morning?"

"Tired. But it's Orangutan Thursday. I'm off to spend the day with another man." I flirted, deliberately putting the previous day's incident out of my mind. "How do you feel about *that*?"

"Well, James may be a very smart, good-looking orangutan," he teased, "but I'm not worried. I think you enjoy conversation too much to leave me for him."

"Hmm…you're right." I planted a lingering kiss on the back of his neck and before I knew it, he'd stood, turned, and pulled me into his arms. His lips claimed my mouth and his body told mine he wanted me to stay.

Breathless, I said, "Well, that's quite a send-off."

"Be safe, Laralee," he said, his voice gruff with emotion. "I need you more than you know."

I reached up and softly caressed his cheek. My eyes filled with moisture as my heart overflowed with tenderness. "I love you, too, Carl."

After holding him close and absorbing the feel of him I whispered, "It's orangutan day—I'll be as safe as if I were here with you."

He released me, and I headed for the door. "See you later, love."

Heading across the compound to the orangutan enclosure, I switched into work mode and pondered the objectives of the experiments. The Spanish government had hired us to design a serum to make the monkeys vicious and extremely aggressive.

Normally pretty good at compartmentalizing, lately, I'd found myself contemplating the monkeys at odd moments. Like now. On my way to work with the orangutans ('tans), I should be enthusiastic and joyful. Instead, I dwelt on how we'd changed the monkeys' diet, feeding the ugly beasts raw meat instead of their usual fruit, insects, and small mammals. I knew the end goal was to create an army of flesh-eating primates that could travel long distances over any type of terrain. It would give Spain quite an advantage over hostile opponents if its army ate the enemy. But I hated it, nonetheless.

Standing on a small rise between buildings, I surveyed the large-animal enclosures and sighed. *I could enjoy the beautiful, tropical island setting if I didn't know what really went on here.*

With no human contact except for the other workers and scientists, I felt completely cut off from the rest of the world. The supply ships that delivered necessities and mail every few months failed to fill the void. I loved my work, but this remote location made it impossible to equally balance career, social, and personal lives.

Descending the small knoll, I meandered through the maze of buildings, storage sheds, and pens, still deep in thought.

We'd made great progress, but I wondered how long we could remain so isolated without turning on each other. Personality differences, power plays, and ego issues made working side-by-side continuously for extended periods of time a questionable endeavor—even though we all professed to be on the same page. The past three years had seemed like a lifetime and I detested the ugly monkeys more with each passing day.

I paused and admired the flourishing garden we'd planted with various flowers, bushes, and weeds. Picking a particularly fragrant bloom, I held it up to my nose, inhaling deeply. This simple pleasure drove thoughts of the monkeys from my mind and I pictured the lovable 'tans.

It was a pleasure working with them. The serum we'd created for these animals had made them smarter, more cooperative, friendlier, and useful to people who needed help.

I imagined the 'tans as gardeners—they'd be great once they learned how to carefully separate weeds from the other plants.

An orangutan butler could answer the door, bring items as requested, and help elderly homeowners up and down stairs.

Construction sites or factories would find them invaluable. Their amazing strength and long arms would allow them to lift and haul things an ordinary human could not. And of course, they wouldn't organize unions, demand health benefits, or ask for a raise.

I smiled as I rounded a corner, thinking again about James. His eyes seemed nearly human and he possessed many child-like characteristics. The fruity smell that clung to him was a welcome change from the fetid, rotten-meat miasma that hovered around the smaller yet infinitely more vicious monkeys.

As a rule, the orangutans' longer reach, larger size, and great strength made them dangerous adversaries, but their friendly, benevolent demeanors ensured they only used their innate power to protect that which they held dear—family, children, and food. They had accepted me as part of the orangutan clan and I knew they would protect me to the death. That had been proven beyond a shadow of a doubt last month.

Stopping in front of the monkey enclosure, I stared at the shiny new lock and shivered as my mind went back to the previous month's debacle. The close call still preyed on my mind.

King Louie, the unofficial leader of the primates housed in Experimental Station #1, had learned how to undo the locks and latches on his cage door. We'd changed them once but had underestimated his growing intelligence. Switching to a combination lock, we'd mistakenly assumed he was securely contained.

One day, as James and I practiced household chores in the wing recently erected between the monkey and orangutan enclosures, King Louie had opened his pen and freed three other primates housed nearby.

While putting dishes into the cupboards, James had whirled, growling. He'd stepped in front of me and I had no idea what was happening until I heard the fierce shrieks and smelled the monkeys' rank odor. I immediately radioed for help and backed to the wall, so they couldn't attack from behind.

Not even realizing I did it, I leaned against the rough wall as I'd done that awful day and continued my ponderings.

James had roared and beat his chest—the orangutan equivalent of "Bring it on!" Rising to his full height, he'd towered over the smaller beasts, but their snarls displayed wicked canines and a defiant lack of fear. My breath had caught in my throat as I'd considered my fate if one of them slipped past James.

A younger monkey leapt in and drew the ape's attention. As he struck at the youngster, the other two darted in on the opposite side.

Horrified by the battle raging before me, I watched James knock the first monkey to the floor as though swatting a tennis ball and turn to Louie and company. One jumped high to his right as another dashed in low to the left, leaving Louie free to pounce on James' unprotected neck.

But before the leader of the ruthless pack could make his move, the door had crashed open and five armed men charged inside. The monkeys had spun to face their new adversaries. James grabbed the nearest one and broke its back, tossing it to the floor like a discarded rag doll.

Louie screeched and ran at the men, waving his arms and baring his teeth. Three *"crrrrraaaaacks"* had left as many monkeys dead.

Immediately, the orangutan had dropped his aggressive posture and turned toward me. Out of the corner of my eye, I saw one of the men raise his gun and take aim.

"No!" I'd yelled, holding up my hand. "Don't shoot!"

James had come to me and put his great hairy arms around my neck, nuzzling my face and blowing puffs of air into my ear—his way of showing affection.

Stroking his back, I'd murmured soft endearments to the animal that had saved my life. If not for him, my blood would've pooled on the floor alongside the other lifeless bodies.

I shrugged off a chill and, putting the memory behind me, opened the heavy-duty padlock, feeling compelled to check on the monkeys. They gave me the creeps. However, a quick look showed all was as it should be, and my nerves settled, so I locked the door behind me and continued to the next enclosure.

My thoughts spun ahead, and I smiled to myself. *The newest orangutan formula appears to be having the greatest effect to date. The injected apes—like James—are eager to help with chores, learn faster and retain more—in fact, if not for the reddish hair, long arms, and lack of speech, it would be almost like teaching human children.*

Standing in the doorway, I watched my favorite pupil. I often gauged James' mood and energy level before entering so I could determine his attitude. 'Tans could be moody—just like people.

How amazing it would be if our next serum could nudge Mother Nature into giving these wonderful apes the ability to speak. We know that the talents of the young often surpass those of the parents, so if not James, then his offspring. We could be that close.

James seemed calm and happy today and I imagined him with Julie, the female orangutan we'd selected as his potential mate. She had also been injected with the newest formula and we expected to start seeing the effects in three or four months. If we saw the results we hoped for...

I can't begin to imagine the intelligence and potential capabilities of this pair's offspring.

I gaped in astonishment as my eyes wandered past James and settled on a new structure. Using the Leggo set we'd given him, he had built an intricately designed castle with a bridge leading to a second, smaller building. Under the bridge "flowed" a piece of blue fabric that resembled a winding river. *He's never seen a castle. How did he...?*

Then I remembered. A kids' picture book I had read to him contained images to go with the story of a knight and his fair maiden. I was anxious to see if their castle resembled this one.

"Good morning, James," I said, opening the door with a flourish.

He rushed to my side for a hug. "Woo-woo. Woo-woo." Excited, he rocked from side to side, pointing to the castle.

"Yes, I see. You've been busy, haven't you?" I walked toward the construction to view the details, glancing around for the storybook. *Where is it?*

The ape took my hand and led me to the sofa, hopping onto the center cushion. He patted the seat beside him and I smiled as I sat. Being read to was one of his favorite pastimes and this was our usual spot to cozy up with a story.

"Where's your book, James?"

He gazed intently at my face.

"Where's your book? Can I see it?"

"Woo-woo-woo!" Jumping off the sofa, he reached underneath and pulled out the hard-cover picture book, adding some excited screechy commentary as he handed it over.

Thumbing through the pages, I soon found it. The castle looked almost exactly like the Leggo one on the floor. Impressed, I said, "Well, aren't you the clever 'tan?"

He pulled back his lips and showed his large, square teeth in a comical monkey-smile.

I couldn't help but grin in return and when he wrapped his long arms around me in an affectionate hug, I tickled his sides. In some respects, he was a big, hairy kid—monkey-giggles and happy screeches filled the air.

During our housework lessons, James continued to amaze me as he vacuumed the room and set the table. We ate a small snack and he then cleared the plates and washed the dishes with little direction from me.

Afterwards, we headed into the garden to pull weeds. He could now differentiate between the flowers and the weeds, knowing which ones to pull and discard, so I decided to try a transplant. Using the shovel, I dug a medium-sized hole, loosened the soil, and added a few scoops of black dirt from the compost pile. Gently digging up a small bush, I showed James how to transplant it, tamp down the soil, and water it thoroughly to give it the best chance to thrive. Focusing his attention on the task at hand, he absorbed the new information like a primate-shaped sponge. I had no doubt he could do the next one by himself.

Eventually, we made our way back to James' room and settled on the sofa to read. I let him select the day's book and wasn't surprised that he chose "The Knight and His Fair Maiden" again. He seemed enthralled with knights, castles, and dragons.

At the end of chapter four, he suddenly hopped off the sofa and went to the kitchen. Curious, I waited to see what he was up to. Glasses rattled, and I heard the refrigerator door open. Ice clinked. A package crinkled.

When James casually strolled from the kitchen bearing a tray containing two glasses of iced tea and a plate of cookies, I nearly fell off the couch. I hadn't taught him to do this.

He carefully placed the tray on the coffee table, never spilling a drop. Offering me a glass of tea, he then held out the plate of chocolate chip cookies. I knew these were his favorites, but he controlled his eagerness and waited until I had taken one before helping himself to three.

I smiled and thanked him before nibbling my cookie. He greedily stuffed two into this mouth, chomped, and grinned hugely, chocolate bits and crumbs caught in his teeth and peppering his lips. Evidently, his manners only extended to waiting for his guest to take a cookie.

Recalling our lessons, I could only surmise that he had extrapolated from past sessions and put two and two together. He loved iced tea; he loved cookies; and he knew I enjoyed them, too. So here we were, munching on tea and cookies spontaneously served by an orangutan! Amazing!

I arrived home that evening, excited and anxious to share James' behavior with Carl and disclosed every detail as we prepared dinner. "Obviously, he's *thinking and reasoning*—using what he's learned in our lessons to alter his conduct. Plus, he's recalling what he's seen me do—I never taught him to use the tray or serve snacks, but I've done that myself many times."

Our enthusiasm spilled over into bedtime and we continued what Carl had begun that morning. On the one hand, I was miserable with the arrangements on our tiny, experimental island. On the other, life was good.

Chapter 3

CARL SENT our request to the Spanish government via the next supply ship. And we waited.

Days passed…then weeks and months. Work continued with the ugly, vicious monkeys and the lovable orangutans and I nearly despaired of receiving an answer. Thankfully, no one else fell prey to the monkeys' increasing appetite for flesh, but I knew that human nature would eventually cause our hyper-vigilance to wane. Someone would become complacent, a bit careless. Someone else would die a horrible death.

I tried not to dwell on how long it had been since we'd submitted our request and kept busy with the experiments. When Julie—our female orangutan of child-bearing age—showed signs of coming into heat, we moved her into James' enclosure. Since both 'tans had been injected with the newest serum, we had high hopes for exceptional future offspring.

In addition to the meticulous experiment notebook I had kept from Day 1, I began logging both animals' behavior and documented the first signs of amorous conduct. They flirted. He courted her. She teased him.

I knew that in the wild, sexually mature males would make what is known as a long-call and wait for potential mates to come to them. The females prefer flanged males—those with cheek pads—to the unflanged, younger and less experienced males who often resort to rape.

Since James was about eighteen years old, had well-developed cheek pads, throat pouch, and the long hair of an adult, sexually mature male, we hoped Julie would find him irresistible and the two might form a lasting relationship.

Two days after we'd moved her into James' enclosure, we heard him long-calling. Rushing to a vantage point where we could see the 'tans without being intrusive, we watched the initial courtship. She responded to his call by strolling past, seemingly unconcerned, to the far side of the pen. He watched her go by like a lecherous old man might gaze at a well-stacked woman at the gym.

We laughed.

The next day when James called, Julie strolled by again, but this time gave him come-hither eyes. After a bit of hesitation—we could almost read his *Who, me?* look—he ambled after her.

They spent one additional day frolicking and chasing, calling and declining, finally seeming to develop a comfortable rapport.

Soon, the nuzzling and sniffing, nipping and groping commenced. Once the initial deed was done, the happy pair seemed oblivious to on-lookers and repeated the enthusiastic coupling whenever and wherever the mood struck. Certain we'd eventually have an infant in our midst, I checked the calendar and marked Julie's due date—approximately nine months hence—and began administering prenatal vitamins. We wanted this youngster to be as healthy as possible.

A month later we performed a pregnancy test to confirm that the mating had been successful. It was positive! The joyous information lifted everyone's spirits and workers often whistled while they went about their daily routines. Laughter once again drifted between buildings.

Although I felt more lighthearted and optimistic at the thought of Julie's and James' sure-to-be-exceptional child, a subsequent incident diminished much of the joy. While working in the lab across the room from where Artie had met his fateful end, the tiny hairs on the back of my neck stood up. I froze. Someone was watching me. I glanced around and met the unwavering stare of three pairs of hostile eyes.

The monkeys that had been shot after assaulting Artie had inhabited the most obvious and accessible cages since they had needed nearly constant observation to monitor behavioral changes.

After the attack, we had selected three new subjects from our small pool of primates. We kept a group of ten additional monkeys—all about the same size and age—in case some became ill, had an adverse reaction to the serum, or became totally unmanageable.

We had moved them into the empty pens and begun the experimental protocol. These monkeys had responded well to the serum and we'd logged an increased appetite for meat, a higher level of aggression, and rapidly growing intelligence.

Today, I saw evil in their eyes—not the hatred animals might display for their captors but pure, intentional malevolence. Icy fingers clawed the entire length of my spine.

The three assumed identical stances, their gazes affixed on me, never moving, never blinking. Their hunger, their desire to rend and tear washed over me in nearly palpable waves although they remained completely motionless. I could smell my own fear.

My radio squawked, ripping into the silence. I shrieked and tossed my clipboard, breaking eye contact and turning away from the cages. The monkeys screeched and yowled, dashing from one end of the enclosures to the other in frenzied, furious movement.

My knees weak, I leaned against a table and keyed the mike. "Laralee, here." My voice sounded strained, on edge.

"Are you alright?" Carl asked. "You sound strange."

"Yes, I'm fine." I let out a deep sigh of relief. "I just had an unnerving experience in Building Two."

"What happened?" he snapped. "Did a monkey escape?"

"No, no, nothing like that." I took a deep breath. "It's just… The three new subjects seem to be progressing more quickly than the previous ones. I could swear I saw evil intent in their eyes." I shuddered and changed the subject. "What did you need?"

"The radio operator received a message today advising that a supply ship will be here next week. I'm hoping we'll get a reply from the Spanish Committee on Scientific Experiments."

"That would be nice—it seems like forever since you sent the request. Thanks for letting me know."

"Are you sure you're okay? Do you want me to come over and help with the afternoon data collection?" His voice deepened, heavy with concern.

"No, I'm fine. It's just a case of nerves. You have your own work to do. I'll see you at home later." We alternated days working with the monkeys and the 'tans and I knew he hated these beasts as much as I did.

I retrieved the previously airborne clipboard and turned to face the cages once again. The monkeys darted to and fro, the earlier malevolent attitude seeming a figment of my imagination. Malignant intent aside, it was clear they wanted their dinner.

Opening the door to the storage room, I prepared their meals, gagging as I heaped bowls with chunks of raw, bloody meat. Once more, I mentally thanked Carl for including a farm worker in our list of necessary employees. The man kept a small herd of cows and some chickens on the other side of the island, supplying us with a ready supply of meat. In addition, he kept *our* freezer well stocked.

The cacophony rose in volume, the screeches nearly loud and high-toned enough to shatter glass, as I returned to the enclosure. I placed one bowl on the conveyor belt we had installed to carry the food into the pens. It simply wasn't safe to get close enough to shove the bowls through the opening at the bottom of the bars. One after the other, the food rumbled into the appropriate cages and the smacking, chewing sounds commenced.

Making notes, I detailed their attitudes: eager, aggressive, hungry, and wrote in what and how much food they'd each received.

Although anxious to leave the repulsive sounds behind, I took a few moments to re-read the entries from the last few days, comparing notes. Everything looked good—no lethargy or signs of adverse reactions. *There's certainly no problem today.*

Feeding them was the last chore I carried out each day so that I could leave the building immediately thereafter. Their wet gnawing reminded me of the sounds they'd made chewing on Artie's arm.

I passed Vicente, a member of the cleaning crew, in the doorway. We smiled and nodded, spoke, and I continued on my way, my thoughts leaving the primates far behind.

Suddenly my radio emitted a high-pitched scream—then... nothing. I whirled and ran back to Building Two. In my gut, I knew it was Vicente. *What have the monkeys done now?*

I found Vicente lying face down in front of the cages in a growing pool of blood. Thankfully, he'd fallen away from the pens—not alongside them—and had had the presence of mind to crawl as far as he could before blacking out.

The monkeys had ripped off one of his ears and deep scratches showed how they'd tried to pull him close enough to bite out his throat. Deep lacerations covered his chest and shoulders. One deep bite bled profusely.

I brought the mike to my mouth. "Medics to Building Two NOW!"

I dragged him another foot away from the pens and applied pressure to the worst of the wounds, flashing back to Artie. *Not again. Please, not again!*

As I worked on Vicente, two of the monkeys wrestled over the ear, each chomping on a piece of the tasty morsel. I fought the urge to vomit.

Unlike before, the pressure stemmed the blood flow and I felt a strong pulse under my palms. As the door crashed open, I yelled, "He's alive! He's alive."

The medics shouldered me aside and administered first aid to stabilize him before lifting him onto a gurney. As they wheeled him out, one EMT turned to me. "You saved his life, Doc. He'll be okay."

Once they'd gone, my knees buckled, and I slid down a wall of cabinets, collapsing into a sobbing heap on the floor. Next to the congealing red puddle, I leaned my head on my arms and knees and cried.

Moments later, Carl gently wrapped his arms around me and whispered soothing sounds in my ear. "Are you okay, Laralee? This blood—it's not yours?"

I looked down at my hands, a crusty, rusty-red. "No, it's Vicente's. I'm alright."

"Come, let's go home and get you cleaned up."

He helped me to my feet and looked searchingly into my eyes. "Are you sure you're not hurt?" Concern filled his voice and he ran his hands up and down my arms as though hunting for tiny wounds that might've caused me pain.

"Yes. I'm fine. I ran back in when I heard the scream on the radio. I found him lying there…" I pointed to the drying pool of blood. "…and radioed for the medics."

"My wife is stronger than she looks," he said, pulling me close again. I could feel him smiling against my hair.

"I felt helpless, but at least they said he'll be alright."

"Do you know what happened?"

"No. Once I wash up and change my clothes, I want to go see Vicente—he should be able to paint a clearer picture of the incident. The more we know about how the attacks happen, the more prepared we can be to prevent more."

Now that I'd stopped trembling, I was anxious to fill in the details.

"Let's go. I need to wash up."

***

Later, clean and more composed, I slowly approached Vicente's room. I'd wanted to come alone, figuring he'd speak more freely. I pushed open the door and entered quietly, but before I could speak, he reached out and took my hand.

"I don't have words enough to thank you. You saved my life."

"There's no need to thank me—I'm just glad you're going to be alright."

"Yes, but I'm sure from now on everyone will call me Vicente van Gogh." A lop-sided grin proved that he may have lost an ear, but he still had his sense of humor.

After a few moments, I broke the silence. "Can you tell me what happened?"

He paused as though collecting his thoughts. "I was careful. I'm always careful around those beasts. But today they seemed…different."

"Different how?"

"Like they had a secret."

I frowned, not understanding. "What do you mean a secret?"

He looked down at the bandages on his chest, avoiding my eyes. "Usually, when I go in after you've fed them, they shriek and chatter and try to protect their food bowls as though they think I'm going to take them away. But today…"

Another pause. "They looked up at me, left their food, and walked to the back of the pens. I remember thinking, *That's odd. But it's nice not to have all that racket.* And I figured if they were going to huddle at the back, I'd sweep in front of the pens while it was safe."

Taking a corner of the sheet in his hands, he rolled it between his fingers. After a deep breath, he said, "This is where it gets really weird." He looked up and glanced around the room like he was sharing something he didn't want anyone to overhear.

"I was sweeping the floor when I heard a wet *splat* across the room. I stopped and looked in that direction and that's when they attacked. They grabbed my shirt, pulled me against the bars, and started biting…"

A sob interrupted his narrative and it was my turn to take his hand. I waited until he regained control.

"What was it you heard, Vicente? The *splat?*"

"I think one of the monkeys threw a chunk of meat across the room, so I'd look in that direction. They wanted me to be standing with my back to them—looking away—while close enough for them to reach me." Again, he glanced around and, in a whisper, said, "They planned it."

I shivered. The room suddenly felt very cold.

"Can they do that?" he asked. "Make plans, I mean." He sounded unsure and afraid.

"If what you say is true and they purposely went to the back of the pen, tossed a chunk of meat to direct your attention, and then attacked while you were most vulnerable, they're thinking. And not only thinking but reasoning and strategizing."

Still fiddling with the sheet, he looked down and then back up, holding my gaze. "That makes them more dangerous, doesn't it?"

"Yes. Yes, it does." *Infinitely more dangerous.*

His face went paler than the stark white bandages covering the side of his head.

My mind in a whirl, I said, "You get some sleep and I'll come back tomorrow, okay? Your body needs rest to heal." I patted his shoulder. "Don't worry about the monkeys."

Outside, I leaned against the doorjamb. If what he'd said was true, the chunk of meat should still be on the floor. It would be proof.

Walking to Building Two, I chided myself for the anxiety that tied my stomach in knots. I unlocked the door and took several deep breaths. Flipping on the light, I expected the usual raucous chatter but was greeted instead with stony silence.

Oh, my God, had they escaped?

Loath to enter without knowing for sure, I peered into the dimness shrouding the cages. Another switch located across the cavernous room would brighten the enclosures, but from here, I couldn't tell if the animals were at the back of the pens or not. I cursed the electrician who had wired the large, poorly lit addition.

Pulling out the tiny flashlight I always carried in my bag, I aimed the beam into the enclosures. From the doorway, it failed to illuminate the far recesses, the deep shadows fully capable of hiding the vicious beasts, leaving me still in doubt about my safety.

I wiped a clammy palm on my pants and placed it on the radio, my thumb on the button, taking a cautious step inside. Listening intently, I strained to hear the slightest sound. There! A rustle. A sigh.

They're there.

I slowly approached the cages, maintaining a respectful distance. *This L-shaped configuration will have to be eliminated at the new facility. The corner allows all three monkeys to be able to reach anyone standing there—that's how they grabbed Artie and Vicente.*

As I peered inside, a sudden screech rent the air. A monkey leapt at the front bars and I stumbled back. He clung to the rails, teeth bared.

My eyes slowly adjusted to the dimness and I could see the other two animals at the rear of their enclosures. They seemed to be watching—and enjoying—their friend's antics and my discomfort.

Now that I knew where they were, I concentrated on my reason for returning. The puddle of blood had been cleaned up, but a faint stain remained. I recalled Vicente's position when I'd found him and gazed across the room. It shouldn't be too difficult to find the chunk of meat if, indeed, that's what the noise had been.

Using a flashlight to illuminate all corners and overhanging edges, I slowly shuffled across the room, surveying every inch of exposed floor. Back and forth—until I spotted a dried trail leading to a chunk of meat nearly invisible underneath a low shelf. I turned and stared at the enclosures, studying the trajectory from here…to there… It led directly to the monkeys' pens.

The dried blood trail clearly showed how the meat had slid. That wouldn't have happened had it merely been dropped.

Vicente was right. It did seem that one of the monkeys had tossed a coveted piece of meat to direct his attention across the room.

I heard a low chatter, a give and take that sounded very much like a discussion coming from the cages. The monkeys stood at the rear, deep in conversation, every now and then raising their eyes to look at me.

They know I've found the meat—and they don't like it. Those icy fingers clawed at my spine once again.

The primates walked slowly and deliberately to the front of the cages, their eyes never leaving mine. Gripping the bars with their hands, they lowered their chins until they stared malevolently from under protruding, bushy brows. As one, their upper lips lifted in a silent, wicked snarl.

The evil threat times three totally unnerved me and I dashed for the door, my hip clipping the corner of a metal cart in my haste. The loud clang sounded eerily ominous in the silence.

Shoving the exit door open, I ran outside and stood there in the fresh evening air, heart hammering, pulse pounding—and heard the monkeys…laughing.

Chapter 4

THE FOLLOWING WEEK, all workers and scientists kept an eye on the horizon, anxiously awaiting the supply ship's arrival. During a time-sensitive data retrieval, a shout filled the air and I saw people running for the shoreline. That could mean only one thing.

"The ship's here," Carl yelled, poking his head in my door. "You coming?"

I raised one gloved hand and motioned for him to go on without me. "I'll join you in a minute."

Peering out the window, I saw him dash away, legs pumping like a school kid eager to greet summer vacation. I smiled. He was a brilliant scientist but occasionally acted like a gangly teenager.

Finishing the paperwork and meticulously recording the data, I, too, then headed for shore. Once every other month or so, all work was suspended—except for the care and feeding of the animals—as we visited with the ship's crew and listened to the latest news and gossip. After working seven days a week, we earned that rare day off. And I was dying to know if we'd received an answer to our request.

Crates and boxes lined the shore where the dinghies had off-loaded supplies from the ship anchored in deeper water. As I watched, two craft sped toward us across the gentle swells, filled with additional containers.

Elbowing my way through the crowd, I spotted Vicente and stopped to speak. "How are you feeling?"

"Hello, Dr. Laralee, much better, thank you. The doctor says the bandage can come off soon. And I was right—they're calling me van Gogh now."

I smiled. "Well, there are worse names."

He snorted. "Yeah, that's for sure." Pausing, he took a deep breath and said, "Do you have a minute? I need to talk to you."

"Sure."

He squirmed uncomfortably, avoiding my eyes.

Finally, I asked, "What is it, Vicente?"

"I don't want to work with the monkeys anymore," he blurted. "If there's nothing else I can do here, I'd like to leave when the supply ship goes." Tears filled his eyes. "I have nightmares every night and get sick to my stomach just thinking about going into Building Two." He lowered his voice and whispered, "If I stay, they'll kill me."

My heart went out to him. He was obviously terrified. "Let me talk to Dr. Carl and see if we can find another position for you. I'll let you know soon enough that you can take the ship home, if need be. Alright?"

He sniffed and nodded. "Thank you. You probably think I'm a terrible coward."

"Not at all. After what you've been through, you have every right to feel the way you do." I put my hand on his arm and felt him trembling through his shirtsleeve. "I'll talk to Dr. Carl. I promise."

I turned and made my way to my husband's side, nudging him none too gently with my elbow. "Well? Did we get an answer?"

Without speaking, he pulled a creamy envelope from his shirt pocket and handed it to me. I envied his ability to maintain a poker face as I nearly ripped the missive in my eagerness.

Yes! They've agreed to move the facility!

Rocking back and forth in excitement, I quickly scanned the brief message. The last paragraph told me what I wanted to know.

We only have six months to draw up plans for the new facility, get them approved, and prepare to relocate.

"Well, Laralee," Carl said, smiling down at me. "You got your way. Are you ready to pack?"

"Yes!" It was all I could do not to hop up and down. "But there's so much to do." My detail-oriented mind was already making lists.

"We don't have to start today. Relax and enjoy the break. You need it as much as anyone. Maybe more."

Just then, a booming voice interrupted our conversation.

"Dr. Carl."

We turned in unison as a big bear of a man ambled our way. He ran his fingers through his too-long, curly grey hair and unselfconsciously scratched a chin hidden deep in his bushy beard. Bright blue eyes sparkled mischievously as his face split into a welcoming smile. One missing front tooth gave an otherwise intimidating countenance a somewhat comical appearance.

"Tiny" Tolliver had captained the original boat bringing supplies to this island over three years ago and since then we'd become fast friends.

Towering over Carl, the mountain rumbled, "Good to see you," and stuck out his hand.

After the men had shared brief pleasantries, Tiny turned to me. "Hello, Lar-lee."

Ignoring my proffered hand, he bent and enveloped me in a bear hug, lifting me completely off the ground. I dangled awkwardly in midair like a five-year-old greeting a favorite uncle.

"Put me down, you big galoot!" I said, pounding ineffectively on his back. "How can I look professional with you acting like this?"

He settled me gently on the sand. "You wouldn't have me any other way, now admit it." His eyes twinkled like cobalt Christmas lights and he winked conspiratorially.

I flushed at his cheekiness and pretended to be offended by his display of affection, but he was right. I recalled how he'd treated me like a daughter when I'd been overcome with seasickness on our initial trip to the island. He'd brought me tea, water, and broth to keep me hydrated and special herbs to settle my stomach. Then I'd spent many hours on the bridge as he'd regaled me with seafaring tales and pointed out dolphins racing the bow. The big bear occupied a special place in my heart.

I melted at his grin, winked back, and admonished, "I have to keep up appearances, you know."

"But I don't," he said. "I am what I am…and everyone knows it."

He eyed the cream-colored paper and official-looking envelope still clutched in my hand. "What's that? It looks important."

"The Committee on Scientific Experiments has agreed to relocate the facility to a larger island. I'm sure you'll be notified of the move soon. In six months, two ships will be sent to load everything—people, animals, supplies, the whole kit-and-caboodle—and take us to the new location."

"Really? That's quite an undertaking. Why are you moving? And where are you going?"

"There's not enough space on this little island for us to work safely around the animals," Carl said. "We need room to expand."

"This didn't say what island we're going to," I said, fluttering the papers in my hand, "just that they've approved our request. That information will be in your notice."

"Looks like we're all going to be busy," Tiny said. "I'm going to go make sure the galley crew is prepping for tonight's feast. Then I'm taking a long, hot shower. In case you haven't noticed," he sniffed and wrinkled his nose, "I'm overdue." He smiled and turned away, waving one hand in the air in a friendly goodbye.

"Perhaps we should check on our chefs, too," I said. "I love our once-every-other-month buffets and the social gathering with the crew. It's kind of like a party." I grinned and slipped my arm through Carl's.

"It is a nice break after keeping our noses to the grindstone for so long. Let's go," Carl said. "They've nearly off-loaded all the containers. There's nothing we can do here."

***

That evening, scientists, facility workers, and ship's crew gathered for a communal meal. Coordinated by all capable chefs and cooks, the food looked scrumptious and smelled even better.

High spirits sparked laughter, conversation, and jokes at every table. Tiny joined Carl and me, sharing his newest seafaring tales and the hair-raising accounts of storms in open ocean. I longed to tell him about our success with the orangutans and Julie's pregnancy, but was bound by our nondisclosure agreement, so the conversation was rather one-sided. He talked, we listened.

When appetites had been satisfied and plates cleared, I stood to make an announcement. After two false starts drowned out by loud guffaws and rising post-dinner babble, Tiny rose beside me and uttered a single word.

"Silence!"

It cut through the din like a crack of thunder. Conversation halted mid-sentence. Laughter faded. All eyes turned my way.

"Thank you, Tiny." I smiled as he took his seat. Various thoughts flitted briefly through my mind before I began.

It seemed that stature and testosterone automatically conferred respect with this crowd—I'd had to fight hard for acceptance and recognition in the scientific community. My diminutive frame had forced me to overcompensate with my intelligence and determination to succeed in a male-dominated field. But at times, an authoritative voice came in handy.

Looking over the group, I said, "I have an announcement to make. The Spanish government has approved our request to relocate Experimental Station #1 to a larger island. In six months, Captain Tolliver and his crew and another ship will arrive to transport us to our new location."

Applause interrupted, and I waited for it to die down. "Carl and I will draft designs for the new buildings and will be meeting with department heads on an individual basis. Please be thinking not only of your current needs, but what you'll require in the future as the experiments progress.

"Now, please enjoy the rest of your evening and get a good night's sleep. We'll be exceptionally busy for the next six months."

I sat to the sound of thunderous applause, hoots, and hollers. Obviously, I wasn't the only one pleased about the move.

Later that night as Carl and I readied for bed, I recalled the conversation I'd had with Vicente.

"I saw Vicente in the crowd this afternoon and he pulled me aside to talk."

"How's he doing?" Carl asked.

"He's healing alright—physically. The bandages will come off soon, but the poor man was trembling as he asked if he could have another assignment. He no longer wants to work with the monkeys. He's absolutely convinced they'll kill him."

Preparing to brush his teeth, Carl stopped, toothbrush in hand. "Do we have another position he could fill?" he asked thoughtfully. "I thought we were fully staffed."

"We are." I sat on the edge of the bed and sighed. "But he's terrified. He said if we can't move him, he'd like to be on the ship when it leaves."

"What did you tell him?"

"I promised I'd talk to you and let him know soon enough that he can be on the ship if we can't reassign him."

I waited while Carl finished his ablutions. We crawled into bed and continued the discussion. We did some of our best talking and decision making in the hour before we shut off the bedside lamp.

"Has anyone else expressed an interest in working with the monkeys?" he asked.

"No. But if Vicente leaves, we'll have to reassign someone else, anyway." I paused, deep in thought, and then continued. "I'd like to move him, if possible. He's a good worker, is conscientious, and is great with the animals. I'm sure he'd love working with the orangutans and it would give him the opportunity to regain his confidence. The attack really rattled him."

Carl turned on his side to face me. "Alright. If we move Vicente to work with the 'tans, who goes over to the monkeys?"

I ran down the roster of orangutan workers in my mind. "Sheila?"

He shook his head. "She wouldn't last a day with the beasts. She's great with the 'tans but doesn't have the guts to work with the monkeys."

"Rufus?"

"He'd be too inclined to mistreat them. He's good with the 'tans because they're sweet and don't bring out the bully in him."

"John?"

"You know he keeps a bottle of Scotch in his locker, right? One nip too many would be the death of him. The only reason I haven't sent him home is because he's good with the 'tans and it would leave us short-handed. We need someone who's on top of things, day in and day out."

"You're right, of course. How about Gustav?"

"Hmm… Maybe." We lay there in silence, each of us considering the pros and cons. Finally, I said, "Let's sleep on it and discuss it in the morning. I don't want to keep Vicente hanging any longer than necessary, but neither do I want to make a mistake. Gustav is a possibility. Maybe we can come up with another option, too. How's that sound?"

Carl turned out the light and reached for me in the dark. "You know I married you for your razor-sharp mind, right?" he asked, nuzzling my neck.

"Hm," I giggled. "If that's true, why is your hand…oh!" I gasped. Conversation ceased.

Chapter 5

IN THE MORNING over breakfast, Carl and I once again debated the ins and outs of rearranging employees and came up with no other viable options. I decided to talk to Gustav. If he was willing to work with the monkeys, I was certain Vicente would stay. Jobs working closely with the monkeys included hazard pay so Vicente would suffer a cut in salary while Gustav would get a raise, however, I doubted that would be a major factor in the decision.

I found the gruff but gentle German preparing the orangutans' breakfast. "Good morning, Gustav. How are you today? And how are the 'tans?"

"Goot morning to you, Dr. Laralee. I am fine. T'e 'tans are finer." He shot me a wide smile, his eyes nearly swallowed up as the wrinkles and creases rearranged his face. Severely overlapping front teeth added to the oddity of the man's smile, but there was nothing odd about his sincerity.

"I have a question for you and I'd like you to consider it carefully before answering."

He put down the fruit bin and turned his attention and ample frame toward me. "It is somet'ing serious?"

"Yes, it is. You heard about the monkeys' attack on Vicente, didn't you?"

He nodded. "Ya. It was terrible."

"He's convinced he will die if he continues to work with them and has asked to be transferred. If we can't find another position for him, he'll leave on the ship tomorrow. Since we're fully staffed, the only solution is to switch Vicente with another worker."

I could see in Gustav's eyes the realization of what I was going to ask.

"You want me to work wit' t'e monkeys?"

"Yes. You would, of course, receive hazard pay and your hours would change. Vicente works the 5-to-1 a.m. shift."

He lowered his gaze and stared at the floor to think.

When he spoke again, his voice contained sorrow, regret. "If I refuse, Vicente will leave and we will be short one, ya?"

"Yes."

"And you will still have to move someone to fill t'e opening wit' t'e monkeys?"

"Yes."

He raised his eyes to meet mine. "T'ere is no one else?"

The sadness in his voice tore at my heart and I put my hand on his arm. "Gustav, I know you love the orangutans and you're very good with them. Dr. Carl and I have discussed it. The 'tans are lovable and easy to care for—that's why there are more people who want to work with them. You would also be good with the monkeys, though, because you're conscientious, alert to their behavior, and would not torment them because they aren't sweet like the 'tans. We think you are the best option for the animals."

Giving that time to sink in, I glanced around the food prep area. It was spotless and well organized. Another good reason he would be the best choice.

He sighed deeply. Resigned? Sad? Probably both.

"Ya. I will do it for t'e animals. And, too, for Vicente. He is a goot man."

"Thank you, Gustav. This is a great help. You can visit the 'tans as often as you like once you're off duty. They won't forget you."

"When do I begin?"

"Tomorrow. You can finish up here today and report to Building Two at 5:00 tomorrow afternoon. I'll be there to walk you through the routine and the safety protocols and show you where things are located."

"Ya," he said with resignation heavy in his voice. "I will be t'ere."

***

Once Vicente had recovered enough to take over some of the less taxing chores, he settled into working with the orangutans while Gustav learned the ropes in Building Two.

Carl and I designed the structures and layout of the new facility, met with department heads, and made changes as differing needs arose.

Before long, satisfied with the arrangement of staff housing, offices, animal enclosures, storage units, and everything else we could think of, we sent the plans to the Spanish Committee on Scientific Experiments via Tiny's supply ship. And again, we waited.

In only a few weeks, the government sent word by our ancient and somewhat undependable radio that our designs and supply needs had been approved. Ships would be loaded with construction materials and builders and set sail as soon as possible. Thrilled at the prospect of a newer, safer work environment, I caught myself humming as I worked.

On one hand, time seemed to stop. On the other, it raced as I threw myself back into the experiments and monitored Julie's pregnancy. Apart from being moody, she seemed to accept being with child as a normal part of life. Her belly grew larger and James developed an endearing habit I discovered quite by accident.

One day, I looked for the tray to carry a snack into the living area while James and I enjoyed reading a new book. It had disappeared. As I searched, wondering where it could possibly have gone, James nonchalantly wandered into the kitchen.

"James, where is the tray? Have you seen it?"

"Woo-woo." He stared at me.

"Does that mean yes, you've seen it or, no, you don't know where it is?" I stopped and put my hands on my hips.

"Woo." He dashed to the door and pointed, out.

"Why do you want to go out? We're going to read…if I can find the darned tray."

"Woo-woo. Woo-woo." He insisted.

Knowing the ape rarely did anything without good reason, I unlocked the door and watched as he ran to the entrance to his enclosure. Puzzled, I followed, hoping Julie was alright. Again, James insisted I unlock the door.

He went to a narrow space between the wall and a cabinet and triumphantly pulled out the mysteriously "missing" tray. He put an apple and a banana on it and carried it to the courtyard where Julie napped in the sun. I watched through a window as he gently talked to her, nuzzled her neck, and offered the afternoon treat. She graciously accepted the food, gazing into his eyes and lifting her lips in a monkey-grin, and bit into the apple while he caressed her bulging belly.

My eyes brimmed with tears at the endearing domestic scene—mom-to-be and doting dad. *I guess I'll have to get another tray. This one's being put to good use.* I wiped my eyes and waited until Julie finished her snack. James came back inside and returned the tray to its narrow spot beside the cabinet.

"Woo."

"Alright, James, you can keep the tray. Let's go back and read our story."

***

Once we received word that construction of the facility was well under way and the ships would come for us in two months' time, we began packing. Each department head was put in charge of his own equipment and materials. Carl and I made regular rounds to ensure every department was progressing at approximately the same rate.

Three years ago, we had disassembled and stored the wooden crates our original supplies had been packed in. Workers rebuilt them, distributing an equal number to each department, although, inevitably, some would ultimately need more than others.

No further supplies would be delivered here, so the cook staff created a menu to last us until the move. Due to the diligence and foresight of our scientific staff, food for the animals, serum for both the monkeys and the orangutans, and prenatal vitamins for Julie had been stockpiled and were not in danger of running out. Our farm worker was instructed only to butcher cows on an as-needed basis. Chickens could be taken for the daily meals.

Big red X's marked off the days on the calendar above my desk, my excitement growing.

Two weeks before the ships were due to arrive, we received a static-filled radio message. An early Atlantic hurricane had wreaked havoc on the western coast of Spain preventing the ships from departing as scheduled. They would keep us apprised of the vessels' new departure date.

My heart sank. Spirits throughout the entire staff dipped after the all-time high of the previous anticipation. Work continued, day in and day out, as we awaited news.

Finally, word came that the ships should arrive in another two weeks. However, the delay had put us firmly into the rainy season and storm after storm—often interspersed with several gorgeous, blue-skied, sunny days—battered our tiny island.

How will the crew be able to load supplies onto the dinghies and maneuver to the ships in this weather? Not to mention sailing to our new location...

My stomach tied itself in knots as I recalled the seasickness that had incapacitated me on the original excursion. I was *not* looking forward to more of that!

Eventually, the skies cleared, and we enjoyed dry weather, taking advantage of the opportunity to pack the last of the crates. The ships were due any time.

As I cleaned out my desk, I picked up the log in which I had noted every detail of the experiments. Thumbing through it, I decided to wrap it carefully in plastic to preserve it from the moisture of being at sea, the humidity in the air, and from the very real probability of rain.

The information contained herein is more precious than any of our cargo—except perhaps for James and Julie and their unborn offspring.

I wrapped it securely and tucked it into a plastic bag that I tied tightly at the top, then slid the packet into the back of the desk drawer. That should prevent water from reaching the paper.

A shout arose outside. The ships had arrived. Butterflies flitted to and fro in my stomach as I joined the throng heading for shore.

Carl and I stood to the side, watching the dinghies motor toward us over the gentle swells. We recognized Tiny in the lead craft and waved.

The gentle giant sauntered over and once again hefted me off my feet. This time, though, I didn't reprimand him. I was too excited to try and act proper.

His news, however, put a damper on my enthusiasm.

"There's a powerful storm heading this direction. We have to load the ships today and get underway as soon as possible so we can skirt the shallow reefs."

Pulling out a topo map, he opened it and pointed to a group of islands a fair distance away. "This is where we're headed—and it'll take about a week to get there—but I doubt we'll make it without running into rough weather. If we can circle to the lee side of one of those larger isles, we can ride out the worst of the storm and proceed when it's safe."

He smiled at the worry I know showed in my eyes.

"Lar-lee, I'll get you and your family there safely—or die trying."

At the word 'family', he glanced at the people standing along the shore and my heart swelled with affection. I included him in that familial group, too, but as I considered the last part of his statement, I shivered.

Carl offered to inform scientists and workers alike of the need for haste and strode from group to group with his message. I overheard his instructions before he moved further away. "Carry everything you can to this staging area and the ships' crew will load it. The animals will go on last."

Everyone scattered, and Carl and I returned to our quarters to collect our belongings. Before long, a veritable mountain of boxes, bins, and bags had accumulated in the sand and people paired off to bring out the heavier crates.

We worked well into the late afternoon. When the shoreline was empty, Gustav and I led the orangutans out, leaving James and Julie for last. They calmly climbed into the dinghies and took seats like odd-looking seafaring passengers in long reddish-orange coats. Gustav and I rode to the ship with them. They were too precious to hand off to the crewmen, no matter how capable they might be. I saw to their accommodations and we returned to shore.

There, everyone who had worked with the monkeys in the last year accompanied Carl and me to Building Two. This was the most dangerous part of the move and I wanted only the more experienced workers involved.

"Vicente, please show Gustav where the wooden panels for the cages are stored," I said. Feed and water bowls, desks, carts, and shelving had already been boxed up. Workers joined forces to carry the refrigerators and freezers outside.

Raucous screeching and chatter from the three most vicious monkeys made communication difficult. Although we'd administered a light sedative to the animals earlier, it seemed to have had little effect. Reluctant to give them more, not knowing how it might interact with the serum, we opted to proceed—carefully.

We slid thick wooden panels, one at a time, into slots built into the metal framework of the cages, preventing the monkeys from reaching through the bars. Without the panels, we wouldn't have been able to get close enough to the pens to carry them to the ship. From the ruckus, it was obvious the primates were not happy about being kept in the dark.

Thank God, Carl had had the foresight to have two sets of reinforced rings securely welded to all sides, one set about a third down from the top and the other a third up from the bottom. Once the panels had been installed, he slipped a heavy metal bar through the top set of rings. On the left and right sides of the cages, they extended two feet on either end, giving the workers a handle with which to carry the pen. The lower rings accommodated a shorter bar for reinforcement. Two bars fortified the top, also, preventing the monkeys from pushing the wooden panel away from the ceiling rails.

With everything securely in place, four of the strongest men hefted one cage and carried it to the shoreline. Two more trips settled the other cages beside the first.

Now for the tricky part—putting a cage into a dinghy and hauling it to the ship. Thankfully, at the moment, the sea was calm.

With my heart in my throat, I watched Carl, our workers, and the ship's crew carefully load monkey #1 into the small craft. Taking their time, they lashed the cage to the cargo rings permanently affixed to the vessel's sides.

As they shoved off from shore, Carl walked to my side and I released a breath I hadn't realized I'd been holding. Then I gasped as a slightly larger swell slapped the dinghy's side. The cage wobbled, and two crewmen leapt to their feet, placing both palms flat on the wooden panels on opposing sides to help maintain the box's slightly top-heavy equilibrium. It didn't help that the enclosed monkey was obviously leaping from side to side, constantly changing the center of gravity.

Several minutes later and without further ado, they arrived at the ship. There, they easily off-loaded the cage with the winch and steel cables.

I exhaled again when the enclosure sat solidly on the deck.

Twice more, the dinghy maneuvered back and forth between ship and shore, safely delivering the screeching cargo.

As the ship's crew stowed the three pens below deck, Tiny rode the small craft back to the beach. "Is there anything else that needs to go?" he asked.

"No." I shook my head slowly as I mentally reviewed each room. "We walked through every building prior to loading the orangutans and the monkeys. All of the furniture and personal items have been loaded." I glanced around at our home-away-from-home. For the most part, it had been comfortable, but I wouldn't miss it. "We're ready."

"Okay, then, let's shove off," Tiny rumbled.

Carl took my hand and helped me into the waiting craft. I smiled gratefully, knowing it would be a while before I got my sea legs. *I'll be glad when we get to the new island. I was born to walk the land, not sail the seas.*

Chapter 6

TINY BARKED ORDERS and the crew smoothly nosed the ship away from the island. In the distance, it appeared abandoned and forlorn. Now, all I could see in every direction was water, but the sun shone in the azure sky, the breeze buffeted my face, and I gratefully drank the herb tea Tiny provided.

The beverage settled the growing queasiness and by later that evening I discovered my sea legs. I had visited the 'tans to be sure all was well with Julie and found the couple seemed to be better sailors than I was.

Although not incapacitated with seasickness, I was still not comfortable knowing the only thing between me and miles of water was a man-made hull. We were in good hands, but if Poseidon and Mother Nature unleashed their powers, could mere mortals save the ships?

For two days and nights we enjoyed clear skies and a breeze that seemed content to push us toward our destination. Jokes and laughter rang out over the sea, dolphins raced the bow and played in our wake, and I saw a whale and her calf eyeing us as we sailed past.

Curious about the animals, I dashed to the bridge, knowing Tiny could answer my questions.

Standing with his back to me, he studied the far horizon with a pair of binoculars.

"Did you see the whales, Tiny?" I asked, breathless from my mad rush from the other end of the ship.

"What?" He turned to me, scowling.

"The whales..." The look on his face stopped me. "What's the matter?"

"I don't like the look of the horizon—there's a storm coming."

"Storm?" I laughed. "It's a gloriously beautiful day." I spread my arms wide and gazed up at the clear blue sky.

"Not over there." He pointed.

I reached for his binoculars. As my eyes focused on the black, roiling clouds in the far distance, I thought again of the miles of water all around us...and beneath.

The whales forgotten, I asked, "What should we do?"

"I'll have a crew member check on the animals and make sure the monkeys are secure. The last thing we need is one of them getting loose in a storm."

I shuddered at the thought. *You don't know the half of it.*

"I don't want to worry everyone needlessly right now, but as the weather starts to deteriorate, I'll have one of the crew hand out life jackets. Tell your people to put them on and go to their bunks. When it gets rough—and it will!—lash yourselves to the most solid thing you can find."

He pulled out a map and shook his head grimly. "The storm's approaching faster than I expected and there's nothing nearby to hide behind—just open water all around. We're on our own."

I found Carl and told him about my conversation with Tiny. We went up on deck and watched the horizon grow steadily darker, although sun still shone on our little portion of the sea.

Crewmen urged the steam ship forward and we zipped over the water so quickly that, for a while, I believed we'd leave the tempest behind.

Then the temperature dipped, raising chill-bumps on my arms. The gentle sea developed an attitude, slapping at the hull, raising us on large swells and rudely dropping us into the resulting trough. Dark clouds marched inexorably across the sky, hiding the once-bright sun. My hopes blew away on the wind that was no longer pushing us toward our destination—it had changed direction and now seemed determined to force us off course.

As rain began falling in torrents, a crew member ran up and thrust two life jackets into our hands. "Put these on and go to your bunks," he muttered, dashing away to deliver more.

We donned the jackets and followed on the crewman's heels, passing along Tiny's directive. "Go to your bunks and lash yourselves to the most solid thing you can find."

After sending all our people to their bunks, I told Carl I'd meet him in a minute and fought my way to the bridge. I asked Tiny for two more life jackets and was shocked when he refused.

"James and Julie are the most precious cargo on this ship. I *have* to do everything I can to protect them!"

"I understand, Lar-lee," he said in a resigned voice, "but I have no more jackets to give you."

Just then, I realized he wasn't wearing a life vest. "Where's *your* jacket?"

He shook his head.

"Tiny! Don't tell me there aren't enough for all the people on board!"

I started unbuckling my vest.

"No! You will *not* take that off!" Tiny gripped my hands and stared hard into my eyes. "Lar-lee, you are the daughter I never had. You will keep your vest and go to your bunk. I swear on all that is holy, I will do everything in my power to get you and yours home safely. Now, go!"

A sob ripped from my throat as I turned away. I looked back, and he was already hard at work, fighting the sea, fighting the storm.

I literally ran into Carl on my way to our bunk. Blinded by rain and tears I never saw him—just felt his strong arms encircle me and pull me to our bunk.

"What is it, Laralee? Are you alright?"

"There aren't enough life jackets for everyone," I sobbed. "Tiny's not wearing one and he won't take mine."

He pulled me close. "You cannot give your jacket away, my love."

I felt his pulse thudding against my cheek, his lips kissing my forehead, rain—or was it tears?—dripping onto my arm.

"Come, we have to tie ourselves in." Leading me farther into the room, he inspected the space and grabbed a coil of rope off the wall. "Here, tie this around your waist."

He tugged the mattress from the bunk, folded it in half, and wedged it between the wall and the post in the center of the cubicle. We crawled inside the padded burrito and he lashed us together, finally tying the rope to the post. Rocking and jerking, rolling and lurching with the storm, we held each other and, surprisingly, fell asleep.

Hours later, a thunderous *crrrrack* and shuddering jolt awakened us. Shouting. Screaming. Thunder and lightning. Waves crashing over the ship. I felt water squishing in the mattress beneath me. *No!*

Suddenly, the ship *cru-u-u-nched* and lurched at an odd angle. And stayed there.

"Laralee, we're sinking! We have to get out of here." Carl tore frantically at the knots he had tied so diligently only hours before.

"Sinking? We have to save James and Julie!" I tried to scramble to my feet but was still tethered to the post.

"Stay still. I have to untie you."

"We have to save the 'tans!"

Taking my face in his hands, Carl said firmly, "We *cannot* go below deck, Laralee. If the 'tans are free, they'll get off the ship. If the monkeys are free..." The unfinished sentence hung ominously in the air between us.

Growling, screeching, and unholy screaming mingled with the mortal groans of a dying ship. Cracking wood and twisting metal underlined the sounds of death all around. The ship suddenly jerked. The angle of the floor beneath us became even steeper and things began sliding, then floating as water gushed into the room.

"Come on!" Carl grabbed my hand. Standing on the side of the bunk, he pushed me up and ahead so I could grab the post. I angled myself around to the far side, leaning against it.

"Can you reach the door jamb?" he yelled over the din.

Scooching around so I stood on the post, I could barely reach the door frame with my fingertips.

"Stay there." Carl pulled himself up to the post with the rope we'd used earlier and stood next to me. Much taller, he was able to heave his body up and out the door, then he reached in and grabbed me with both hands, yanking me up beside him.

We fought our way to the deck and found the nightmare continued there. All three monkeys had escaped and left behind gruesome evidence of their encounters with humans. Flashes of lightning illuminated blood-splattered images I knew I'd never forget. Gore made the deck slippery until the next wave washed it away. The awful sounds… The horrible sights… The foul smells…

I peeked around a corner and thought I glimpsed Julie leaping into the raging sea but couldn't be sure. *Is she any safer there?* My mind stopped processing the horrific scene before me and it almost seemed like an old, black and white movie—except for the splashes of red.

Carl's voice in my ear startled me from my trance. "Come, this way." He led me away from the abattoir, carefully choosing his steps and handholds, bracing me against his body as he battled the lurching ship beneath us. At the rail, he said as matter-of-factly as possible, "We must jump, Laralee."

I looked at him like he'd said we were going to fly to the moon and shook my head in disbelief.

"Yes, love. It's the only way."

"No, no, I can't…" One glimpse of the churning black water below and I backed away, my mind imagining the depth of the water surrounding us. "No, no…" My voice rose in panic and I slapped at his hands when he reached for me.

Suddenly Tiny screamed my name. *"Larrrr-leeeeee!"*

I whirled as the big, bear of a man launched himself at the monkey right behind me, poised to pounce. His momentum threw the primate against and through the already fractured rail. Both plummeted toward the angry sea.

"Noooooo!" I screamed and sobbed as they disappeared into the blackness.

Before I fully realized that Captain Tiny Tolliver had given his life to save mine, a vicious screech came from behind us.

Without looking back, Carl threw his arms around me and leapt off the ship. As the turbulent sea closed over our heads, I thought, *This isn't how my life is supposed to end! We still have important work to do.*

***

I flailed and kicked, water above and below, blind in the darkness. When our life jackets and Carl's powerful kicks forced us to the surface, I fought and struggled like a madwoman, unwilling to die. *I can't quit… I won't give up…*

When my gentle, loving husband slapped me, I stopped, my fist raised in mid-swing, shocked that he would do such a thing.

"Laralee, my love, I am so sorry," he said against my ear, "but you *have* to listen to me. Your vest won't let you sink and I will not let go of you. I promise, I swear, I will *never* let you go. Do you hear me? I will *never* let you go."

I nodded and choked as we bobbed and swirled in the foaming sea, waves breaking over our heads.

"I'm going to turn you around so you're on your back. I will *not* let go of you. Please don't struggle."

I nodded again, although every cell of my being ordered me to fight. Forcing myself to remain still, I let Carl turn me over. Staring upwards, I couldn't tell where the ebony water ended and the dark clouds and sky began.

With rain battering us relentlessly, lightning exploding all around, and waves carrying us high and then dropping us low, Carl did his best to keep me safe. Terrified, I tried not to hinder his efforts and recalled that he'd been a competitive swimmer in college and taught Lifeguard Rescue classes after graduation. I was in good hands—and tried not to think what might be swimming in the water below.

It seemed like forever that the storm and the darkness and the water battled for possession of our souls. Just when I'd swallowed all the salt water I could stomach and thought this nightmare would never end, Carl uttered the most beautiful words I'd ever heard.

"Stand up, Laralee. Hurry, before the next wave comes."

He grabbed my arm and none-too-gently yanked me upright. Waterlogged, choking on saltwater, and weak from fear, I staggered a few steps before the next breaker hit from behind. I flew forward, landing face down in the sand.

Carl dragged me farther up the beach and collapsed beside me. I gagged and retched copious amounts of seawater onto the shore.

Finally, the heaving stopped. "Turn over, honey," Carl murmured. "Open your mouth to the rain—it'll help wash the salt from your tongue."

I did as he said, opening my mouth to the deluge from the sky. Swishing the water over teeth and gums washed away the strong salty taste and I spit the first mouthful out onto the sand. Swallowing the second, I could feel my brine-shriveled cells absorbing the fresh rainwater like tiny, parched sponges.

Too exhausted even to move, we lay there in the downpour, flotsam swept up onto the shore. When the torrent eased to a soft drizzle, we rose on shaky legs and moved to a spot under a nearby palm tree.

Carl sat with his back against the trunk. I snuggled between his legs and leaned on him, his arms wrapped around me like a protective cloak. When I shivered, he held me tighter.

"Cold?" he asked.

"Cold…and terrified. What are we going to do?"

He paused. "Right now, we're going to rest and regain our strength. In the morning, we'll see how many others survived the wreck and take it one step at a time."

His lips brushed my cheek. "Rest, my love. You're safe now. I'll never let you go."

Wrapped securely in my husband's arms, his lips against my hair, my body surrendered to physical and emotional exhaustion. I slept.

Chapter 7

THE NEXT MORNING dawned bright and sunny with no hint of the catastrophic storm. Birds chirped and squawked in the foliage overhead, happily announcing a new day.

I squirmed and squinted at the sunlight glaring off the water. Waves pounded the beach and I wondered how we'd made it to shore.

Some distance away sat the abandoned hulk of our ship, hull submerged, the stern jutting toward the sky.

Carl groaned. "I have to get up, Laralee. This tree has left a permanent impression in my back."

We staggered to our feet and stared at the wreckage. Chills ran up and down my spine as I recalled the previous night's horror, hearing the screams, the tumultuous storm, and the groans of the dying ship in my mind. Puzzled, I asked, "Why is it sitting at such an odd angle?"

"I imagine we hit a reef and tore a hole in the bow. That's why the front went down first. From that angle, the stern's probably resting on rocks."

Lost in the terrible memories, we shared a long silence. Then my thoughts turned to the 'tans.

"I think I glimpsed Julie leaping from the ship." Turning to Carl, I said, "I hope she and James and the baby are safe…wherever they are."

Tears welled in my eyes and formed wet tracks on my cheeks as I thought of another life lost. "Poor Tiny. He saved my life."

"Yes, he did. He loved you, you know."

I nodded, looking down at the sand as a lump lodged in my throat. Swallowing hard, I said, "When I tried to give him my life jacket, he told me I was the daughter he never had." Gazing up into Carl's eyes, I said, "I loved him, too."

Sobs wracked my body. Carl held me and let me cry until hiccups replaced the tears.

Just then, a shout intruded on my misery. "Alloooooo! Alloooooo! Can anyone hear me?"

It's Gustav!

"Over here!" I yelled. "Gustav, we're over here!"

Carl and I ran toward the German's welcome voice. After sharing enthusiastic greetings, I asked, "Are you okay? You're not hurt?"

"No, I am bruised and very sore, but not'ing is broken. I was very lucky."

"Have you seen anyone else?" Carl asked.

"No, I just now began to call. You are t'e first."

"Alright," Carl said, "we should search the area for other survivors and see if anyone needs medical attention. We can possibly treat minor injuries without a first aid kit, but we won't be able to handle anything serious."

A faint cry came from further up the beach. As one, we turned and dashed toward the sound. Rounding a slight bend in the shoreline, we found Sheila, one of our orangutan workers, sitting with a badly wounded crew member. She sat on the sand with the man's head cradled in her lap.

His eyes were closed; hers brimmed with tears.

"Oh, thank God you're here," she whimpered. "I don't know what to do to help him. He's had a hard time breathing and a few minutes ago, he passed out."

Gustav knelt next to the prostrate man and asked Sheila, "Do you know his name?"

"Last night he told me it was Manuel. I think he has a wife and kids."

Gustav opened the man's shirt and gently palpated his horribly bruised stomach and side. Then he leaned down and placed his ear next to Manuel's mouth.

"He has many broken ribs. Probably a punctured lung from t'e sound of his breat'ing. T'ere is not'ing we can do."

"We can't just let him die," Sheila protested, anger sparking in her eyes.

"He has internal injuries that we have no way to treat," Carl said gently. "He's unconscious and probably won't last much longer. Come." He offered her his hand. "You've done all you could. You stayed with him throughout the night—he wasn't alone."

"I'll stay," I said, sitting next to Manuel. I took his hand—he may be unconscious but could possibly be aware of human contact on some other level.

Carl helped Sheila to her feet. With a grim nod at me, he led her to a rock closer to the water with her back to us. Gustav stayed.

"You seemed like you knew what you were doing when you examined him, Gustav," I said. "Were you a doctor?"

"Ya, but not for people. I was a veterinarian for many years in Germany before we came to t'e U.S." He smiled wryly. "I like animals better t'an most humans—t'ey don't argue or criticize and are always grateful for kindness."

"No wonder you were so good with our animals. You weren't a vet in America?"

"My German training and credentials didn't match wit' U.S. requirements. I would have needed anot'er year of school plus an internship and we didn't have t'e money, so I worked as a vet tech, an assistant." He sighed. "Sometimes it was frustrating not to be able to help as I knew I could. But now..." He shrugged and gazed around. "...what difference does it make?"

We fell silent and turned back to Manuel. His breathing had become more labored and bloody froth bubbled from the corner of his mouth. A few minutes later, the wheezing stopped altogether.

"He is gone," Gustav said quietly. After a moment of silence, he added, "We must find a way to bury him."

When Carl glanced our way, I shook my head. He spoke to Sheila and she burst into tears.

A few minutes later, my husband and a still-sniffling Sheila joined us next to Manuel's body.

"We should bury him, ya?" the German suggested.

"Perhaps we should begin by searching the beach for other survivors and see if anyone needs first aid," Carl said. "There might also be other bodies to bury and we could put them all together. We don't have tools so digging may be difficult."

As depressing as that sounded, it was the best we could do. The four of us walked along the shoreline, skirting the debris that had washed up on the beach. A battered metal bucket caught my eye and I picked it up. It would surely come in useful.

We took turns calling, "Hello? Is anybody there?"

We located one other body, a maintenance worker from our experimental facility, and had nearly given up hope of finding anyone else alive when a voice rang out. "Over here! Oh, thank God, more people!"

A bedraggled group of four men and three women—some from our facility, including Vicente, and a few crew members from the ships—had taken refuge at the edge of the jungle. We discovered then that both vessels had perished in the storm. No one had escaped, no one would be sending help.

Once we'd ascertained that everyone in the group had suffered only bruises and abrasions, we fanned out and searched for additional survivors. Shortly after beginning the quest, one crew member made a grisly discovery.

With the water gently lapping at the sole of its shoe, a leg protruded from between two rocks. The sailor turned away and retched after realizing the leg ended just above the knee in a raw wound, white bone extending several inches beyond the jagged flesh.

My eyes met Carl's as he swallowed forcefully and picked the leg up by the shoe. I silently thanked God for giving me a brave and stalwart husband as he carried the limb back and laid it next to Manuel's body.

Carl paused and reached again toward the severed limb. "This looks like a shark tooth." He gingerly plucked a nasty, triangular-shaped object from the irregular wound and held it up for us to see.

The implications were clear. We would have to be careful going into the water since, obviously, sharks inhabited the area around the island.

We continued to search for survivors and/or bodies and a while later, discovered one other partially devoured corpse. We were unable to discern its identity due to horrific damage to the head and face and, in addition, the body was missing the better part of both legs and the right arm from just above the elbow. The jagged wounds left no doubt as to the cause.

Further searching yielded no other bodies and we decided to find a suitable place to bury the dead. We were afraid if we dug a grave too close to the shoreline, high surf would eventually uncover the bodies. Under the trees, though, there was little dirt between the thick, exposed roots, so using flat rocks, the six men took turns carving a burial place out of the rich soil at the edge of the jungle.

Once the bodies and the leg had been laid to rest, we covered the fresh, loose earth with a mound of rocks. Not knowing what kinds of animals lived on the island, we didn't want carnivores finding an easy meal.

By the time the sun rose high into the midday sky, the dismal job was finished, and we desperately needed food and water. Once again, we fanned out, hunting for fresh water and anything edible.

Soon, the tropical sun took its toll, the heat and humidity sapping every ounce of energy I possessed. "Carl, I'm going to sit for a minute. You go ahead; I'll catch up."

Soaked with sweat and weak from hunger, I'd no sooner sat on a log than I heard a shout.

"Over here! I found a stream!"

Energized at the mental vision of cool, fresh water, I leapt up and ran toward the voice.

The group converged at the edge of a wide, burbling stream dancing over rocks and splashing into a clear, shallow pool lined with boulders. In moments, we'd waded into the water and stretched out, allowing the cool wetness to bathe our salt-encrusted bodies.

Too thirsty to worry about whether it was truly safe to ingest, I cupped my hands and drank. Afterwards, I rolled onto my stomach. Here, in less than a foot of water, I felt comfortable enough to completely submerge face and head to remove the itchy, grainy salt left by the sea.

Carl carefully crept around the splayed bodies and sat on a large rock near my head, water rippling over his tennis-shoe-clad feet. "Feel better?" he asked.

"Immensely!" I grinned. "Now, if only we could find something to eat." Just then my stomach gave a great imitation of a large jungle cat.

"I guess we'd better start looking for something edible before you take a chunk out of my leg," he said jokingly, pivoting on the rock to move his long limbs out of reach.

Another shout sounded from amongst the trees. "I've found fruit! Over here!"

The pool erupted in splashing and groaning as everyone tried to stand at once. Shoes squishing, droplets flying, we scurried into the jungle.

Gustav stood in a small clearing holding ripe, yellow bananas and fresh mangoes, the stickiness around his mouth proof that he hadn't waited.

Nothing had ever tasted better. We ate our fill and scoured the area in search of additional edibles, adding coconuts to the menu. Later, we returned to the stream, unwilling to stray far from the life-saving wetness.

My husband, the organizer, called a meeting. "Everyone, please move closer so we can discuss our situation. I'd like input from everybody and we should find out what skills we have among us."

Our group of six men and five women rearranged their seating.

"First of all, is anyone injured badly enough to need first aid?" Carl began.

A plump, mid-forties woman who had worked at the facility performing inventory and accounting raised her hand. "My name's Teresa and I think I have a sprained wrist. It's not broken but it's painful and I can't grip anything."

Gustav went to her and gently checked the wrist. As he flexed it, she said, "Ouch! You oaf, I told you it hurts. What do you think you're doing?" Pulling away from him, she raised her voice and addressed Carl.

"Is there someone else who can examine me? He's just making it worse."

I think more to humor the woman than anything else, Carl again addressed the group. "Do we have any doctors among us?"

When no one responded, he said, "I'm sorry, Teresa, but Gustav is the best we have."

She snorted. "I bet he's not even a doctor," she said, giving the German a look of contempt.

"You are right," he said kindly. "I was a veterinarian for many years in Germany and graduated from one of t'e finest schools in t'e country." He smiled. "So, if you would prefer t'at I not help, t'at is your decision."

He turned to walk away.

"Wait! You have to do *something*."

Gustav turned back to her. "Very well. I will do what I can," he said, reaching for her wrist. "However, you will please call me Gustav, not oaf."

Teresa at least had the decency to blush a brilliant red as she said, "Yes, of course…Gustav." Then, as he wrapped her wrist and made a sling from the sleeves ripped from his own shirt, she added in a much kinder voice, "Thank you."

"Does anyone else need first aid?" Carl asked.

Vicente replied with a question of his own. "Should those of us with severe bruises soak them in the water? Wouldn't the cool water help?"

All heads swiveled toward Gustav.

"Ya, it would help. We have no ice, but cool water is t'e next best thing. Be sure t'e bruising is submerged." He turned to Teresa. "T'e water would help wi't t'e swelling in your wrist, also."

"Alright, those of you with bruises and swelling, please move into the water," Carl said. "The rest of you, gather at the edge of the stream and we'll continue the meeting."

Once everyone had shuffled into new positions, he began again. "We now know that Gustav is our only source for medical attention and although he is not a human doctor, he knows more about treating injuries than the rest of us.

"Let's each state our vocation, skills, and any hobbies we have had that could prove useful to the group in our current situation."

As each person spoke, my high hopes diminished. We had one veterinarian, a chef, two commercial fishermen, a sharp-tongued accountant, several scientists with few other skills, two sailors, and two men who seemed to have few talents or interests—although one claimed to have been an engineer of sorts. He could possibly prove useful. And one was an arrogant former Boy Scout.

Teresa and a plain-but-very-pleasant middle-aged woman named Caroline both had teenaged children, so I knew they possessed the skills required to run a household.

I cringed as I examined what I could offer the group. For many years, I had immersed myself in my studies. After earning a doctorate, I'd worked non-stop and married a colleague, learning few other useful skills or developing hobbies. I'd never had the time. Heck, I could barely cook.

Carl's voice pulled me from my introspection as he addressed the group. "We need to build a shelter for protection from the weather, but we have a couple of options. Do we settle near the beach where we washed up, hoping a ship will sail by to rescue us? This looks like the windward side. It's very rough even on a calm day and is exposed to storms. Or do we find a more protected location on the lee side? What do you think?"

Everyone shouted at once.

Carl raised his hands and called for silence. "One at a time, please." He pointed to Vicente.

"I think we should stay here. What if a ship sailed by and we were on the far side of the island? We'd never see it. We could be here forever."

The shouting began again.

Once more, Carl raised his hands. "Quiet, everyone! I'd like to ask the sailors what they think we should do."

All eyes rested on the two crew members.

Obviously uncomfortable in the spotlight, one burly man squirmed. "Well...it depends on if this side of the island faces a shippin' route. Just because we washed up here, don't mean another ship'll come by."

He looked at his comrade and the man nodded. "We blew off course, fer sure, and don't know where we are. Either side of the island is a crap shoot. We could stay here and miss ten ships sailin' by on the other side." He shrugged. "Then again, we might not be nowhere near a shippin' lane in which case there could never be no ships a'tall."

The silence roared in my ears. *No ships? Ever...?*

"Okay, let's take a vote," Carl said. "Everyone in favor of staying on this side of the island, raise your hand."

I counted eight.

"With eight in favor of staying here, that only leaves three who want to move. So, let's scout the most protected area a good distance from the beach. We don't want to be washed away during the next storm."

After we'd searched the lay of the land for about fifteen minutes, the former Boy Scout, Bruce, approached Carl and me with a comment and know-it-all attitude. "Any location on this side of the island is going to be a disaster. As you can see…" He turned and pointed. "…the beach gradually slopes upwards toward the tree line. Then the jungle continues to slant up that mountain. This side has obviously been battered by storms for a hundred years. The next big blow will hit us hard and we'll have no protection whatsoever. Just sayin'…" He turned to walk away.

"Wait a minute," Carl called.

Bruce turned back.

"So, you think we should move to the far side of the island?"

"Definitely," he said, arrogant in his conviction. "We have no protection here, except for what we build. And how strong can a structure be when we have no hammers or nails, screws or cement? We're asking for trouble."

Deep furrows lined Carl's forehead as he pondered the comments. Finally, he seemed to reach a decision.

"Everyone," he hollered. "Gather round again, please."

As the troupe collected, he said, "I've been thinking, as well as talking with more members of the group. If we set up camp on the other side of the island…"

Grumbling began and interrupted his sentence.

He held up his hands. "Hear me out, please." After the griping stopped, he said, "We could set up camp on the other side of the island in a more protected location and find a spot higher up…" He pointed up the mountain. "…to watch for ships. If we found a ridge that allowed a 180-degree view, we could take turns keeping watch and figure out how to signal a ship if one comes by. We'd be safer away from this exposed beach."

He paused to let that sink in.

"I just don't want to lose any more people," he said. "It would be safer on the other side. What do you think?"

Again, Vicente commented. "I'd be okay on the other side of the island as long as we have a wide view to watch for ships. I don't want to live out the rest of my life here."

Others nodded, and the general attitude grew more positive. Various voices spoke up.

"Okay."

"Let's do it."

"Sure, let's go to the other side."

Numerous people picked up walking sticks and we formed a queue to trudge along the tree line. Bruce took the lead; Carl and I dropped back to the tail end. I imagined Bruce in his Boy Scout uniform—a much younger, cocky, know-it-all. Not much had changed except his age and attire.

Maintaining a comfortable pace, we stopped occasionally for rests and snacks. Fruit grew abundantly here and in addition to the bananas, mangoes, and coconuts, we found papayas.

Colorful birds of all sizes and shapes chirped and squawked, tweeted and whistled above our heads. Well-fed rabbits scampered away as plentiful squirrels and chipmunks darted up tree trunks. Once, I heard snorting in the brush and pictured a wild pig. Looking upwards at a swishing sound in the leaves, I could swear I saw a monkey swinging from limb to limb high in the canopy. I shivered as my thoughts immediately went to the experimental monkeys. Had they escaped? Were they out there? Hunting? Trembling, I looked around, half expecting to see eyes peering back at me from the shadows.

Stop it! I chided myself. Wildlife abounded, and I guess if we were going to be stranded somewhere, this was as good as it gets. There was plenty of easier prey for the monkeys.

After plodding steadily for nearly two hours, we heard a triumphant shout from the head of the line. We dashed to the fore to see what had caused the excitement.

A natural rock formation extended nearly to the beach, forming a sheltered expanse perfect for our needs. A sandy shoreline ranged from the gentle surf to the edge of the jungle—there, sparsely spaced trees allowed sunlight to penetrate. Further in, the trees grew denser, their canopy blocking the sun and creating a shadowy realm, the floor thickly carpeted with leaves and many years of organic debris. A stream burbled conveniently a short distance away. It was perfect.

We rested and discussed the layout of our shelter. Assuming...hoping...praying we wouldn't be there long, we opted for one larger, dorm-like structure rather than individual lodgings.

By nightfall, we had erected a crude shelter large enough to comfortably sleep all eleven with three sides and a thatched roof to keep out most of the rain that was sure to come. When we each claimed our sleeping space, I realized someone was missing.

"Who's missing? There are only ten of us," I said.

Everyone looked around. Guillermo, one of the sailors said, "Jasper's not here."

"Did anyone see him leave?" I asked. "How long has he been gone?"

The sailor snorted. "He left earlier. Anythin' to get out of workin'. He'll come back soon—the work's done."

No sooner had the words been uttered than Jasper strolled into the shelter. He announced, "I found the perfect lookout. It has almost a 180-degree view and isn't too hard to climb to. Even the snooty woman with the sprained wrist should be able to handle it." He stared pointedly at Teresa.

"Who are you calling snooty, you lazy snake?" she retorted.

"Lazy?" He spouted. "Everyone wanted a lookout and now you have one." As he stretched out on the ground, I heard him mutter, "Ungrateful bitch."

This could get ugly. I'd better keep an eye on those two.

Chapter 8

I SLEPT LIKE THE DEAD for several hours, then tossed and turned the rest of the night, convinced I heard monkeys in the trees. Unused to sleeping on the ground, I vowed to soften the earth beneath me and sort out the pebbles before experiencing night number two.

We settled into life on the island as best we could and established a schedule for ship-watching. Although how we could call it ship-watching when there were never any ships to watch, I don't know.

Jasper's suggested lookout was, indeed, perfect. It allowed a panoramic view of the ocean and on a clear day, it seemed we should be able to see distant land masses—but there was only water...everywhere.

Surprisingly, I noticed Gustav spending an inordinate amount of time with Teresa. After their rocky start, things seemed to have smoothed out considerably. She lost her snooty attitude, became downright pleasant, and once her wrist improved, would help anyone who needed it.

Except Jasper.

Those two mixed like oil and water and always had a snide remark for each other. He was one of the laziest people I'd ever met and worked extremely hard at not working. Any time physical labor was involved, he'd disappear into the jungle and reappear as if by magic as soon as the work was done. I suspected he'd built a nest in one of the trees and kept an eye on our little village, knowing exactly when to return. He'd usually bring fruit back with him—a poor excuse for his absence—but eventually we longed for something more substantial and he started coming back empty-handed.

I swear if a cow had crossed my path, I would've throttled it with my bare hands if it meant steak for dinner. And evidently, I wasn't alone in my gastronomic yearnings.

One day, Guillermo and Bruce crafted spears out of slim tree branches and announced, "We're going fishing—we can't stomach any more fruit."

Bored with our daily routine and the frequent squalls, and excited at the prospect of something different to eat, the entire party gathered at the shore with them.

As the men were about to wade into deeper water, I recalled the shark tooth, the severed leg, and the partially consumed corpse. "Wait!" I ran out into the shallow waves and explained my unease, suggesting they hunt in the water around the rocks nearer the beach.

Just then, we heard shouts from Jasper on lookout duty.

A ship?

I shielded my eyes with my hand and saw Jasper frantically waving and pointing—not out to sea, but down near the shore. I couldn't decipher what he was yelling, but as I scanned the water, several fins broke the surface not far from where we stood, knee-deep.

I screamed and pointed. The three of us dashed back to the sand and watched the sharks methodically patrol the shoreline.

"No fishing out there," I said breathlessly.

They didn't argue.

During every high tide, pools formed amongst the large rocks near shore. We investigated and found that fish became trapped, freed when the tide rose again later. Temporarily unable to escape in their limited space, they became easy targets for our homemade spears.

After much flailing and many near misses, Guillermo and Bruce speared enough for dinner. Sushi. My stomach roiled at the thought of eating raw fish, but if I could get the first bite down, perhaps the rest would follow. I needed the protein—we all did. Fruit kept us from starving but hardly fulfilled the recommended minimum daily requirements from all the major food groups.

If only we could cook it.

I envisioned a lightly breaded, perfect fillet sizzling in the skillet, a fresh side salad drizzled with Italian vinaigrette on the table, and a glass of wine waiting to wash it down. My mouth watered. *Stop it!*

While we'd been engrossed in fishing, some of the others had caught a good number of sizeable crabs, using a T-shirt tied shut as a holding tank. *Hmm...a raw food buffet.*

During our walk back to camp, Guillermo told me that in addition to being an avid fisherman, he had trained as a chef. He'd been Tiny's personal choice as head cook on his ship, had fed the crew well, and offered to create a sumptuous meal for us out of our fresh catch.

I noticed that Sheila offered to assist him in preparing the meal and caught the flirtatious glances flying in both directions. Much giggling accompanied the fish-cleaning and preparation of a fruit marinade.

Although some of the men had been carrying pocketknives when the ship had gone down, none were large enough to be useful. As a result, we became inventive at crafting the tools we needed from rocks and tree limbs and the pocketknives helped in carving points on spears.

A razor-sharp fillet knife would've come in handy tonight, though. Thin slices of fish would go down much easier than bite-sized chunks of raw flesh. My stomach flip-flopped again.

Later, when Guillermo announced that dinner was served, we gathered around our makeshift dinner table—a collection of large rocks shoved into a circle. Flat rocks served as our plates. At least we didn't have to worry about chipping the china.

Surprisingly, our self-appointed chef had created a feast despite working without a stove. He and Sheila had shredded the crab and put together a salad of sorts by combining the crabmeat with a variety of greens collected from the jungle. Fruit juice served as dressing.

The sushi, too, was shredded and mixed with tiny bits of fruit and nuts Guillermo had been surreptitiously collecting—the mixture was then wrapped in leaves, creating a very attractive presentation. Everything looked delicious.

He made one announcement prior to serving the meal.

"Please watch for tiny bones in the fish. Without a filletin' knife, I don't know if I got 'em all."

I gingerly placed a small bit of salad on my tongue and waited for my stomach to rebel. Instead, my mouth watered and I chewed with gusto. *It's good!*

With much less trepidation I tested the wrap and discovered our very talented chef had, indeed, concocted a delectable banquet. No one spoke as the meal commenced. We would no longer be existing solely on fruit.

***

Time passed. Our lookouts hadn't glimpsed a single ship and we began to entertain the depressing thought that we might not be rescued after all. In addition, we'd been hearing more treetop activity and primate screeches—especially at night.

Gustav and Teresa and Guillermo and Sheila had become couples. Vicente had been spending a lot of time with Angie, a very attractive woman with long blonde hair and a toothpaste-white smile, but I'd seen Jasper giving her the eye, as well. I felt it was only a matter of time before the two men came to blows.

After six depressing months of day-in-and-day-out ship-watching, we came to the inevitable conclusion that a shipping route ran nowhere near us. We hadn't even seen an airplane fly overhead—at least, nothing close enough to signal. Those faint specks way off in the sky-blue distance hardly counted. So, Carl and I called another meeting to address something that had been preying on our minds.

"We've settled in well and survived the rainy season. I'm proud of everyone for your efforts. Thank you." He smiled at the curiously expectant expressions.

"However, the communal living space is no longer as convenient as it was initially. I think it's time we consider erecting something more substantial."

The grumbling started. And just then a loud screech sounded from high above in the canopy. Leaves rustled and I pictured dark, smelly bodies swinging from branch to branch, tree to tree…watching us?

I shivered as Carl held up his hands for silence.

"Hear me out, please. We can continue to hope for rescue, of course, but we must face reality. I'm sure Gustav and Teresa, Guillermo and Sheila, as well as Laralee and myself, would like our own private spaces. The college dorm has lost its charm." Again, he smiled at the group. Many now nodded in agreement.

"I suggest we build a row of…huts sharing a common wall—for safety's sake—in a row along the shore near here. We can live either individually or as couples. We can continue to use our current building as a communal meeting and eating space but can then retire to our private quarters at night. There's no lack of wood and we can work together to build one hut at a time until we're done. What do you think?"

Gustav stood. "I t'ink it is a wonderful idea. Teresa and I are a little old to go sneaking off to t'e jungle for private time. And she doesn't like t'e bugs."

Teresa blushed as everyone chortled.

Guillermo stood as Gustav sat. "Sheila and I would like our own home, too."

As he flushed pink and plopped back down on his rock, Vicente stood and made a surprising announcement. "Angie and I would like to move in together. We're going to be parents. We're pregnant."

Cheers and whistles sounded from the group and when silence fell again, he added a request.

"Gustav, as our resident doctor, I hope you'll help me keep an eye on her. I've never done this before."

The German nodded. "Ya," he said thoughtfully. "And since she does not have four legs, neither have I, young man, but I will do my best."

Laughter exploded all around as everyone rose to congratulate the young couple.

Carl and I stood off to the side and watched the cheerful group, his arm around my waist. Many thoughts raced through my mind. *Will Angie carry a healthy child to term here on this island? Will a veterinarian be able to deliver the baby without complications? What if…what if…?*

I glimpsed movement out of the corner of my eye and glanced toward the jungle. Jasper strode angrily toward the trees then stopped and turned. Even at this distance, the raw lust I saw on his face as he stared at Angie frightened me. He wasn't one to deny himself what he wanted and now that

Vicente had made his and Angie's relationship—and pregnancy—public, I didn't know what he might do.

Vicente's announcement effectively ended the meeting, but it seemed that most of the group—and certainly, all the couples—had agreed with Carl's suggestion. In speaking with the men individually, they decided to begin work on the huts immediately and I saw nearly everyone walking along the shore scrutinizing various locales.

Carl and I strolled, hand in hand, discussing the pros and cons of the different locations. We found two spots we especially liked and headed back to the communal space to create a drawing in the sand. As each hut was selected, it would be marked off so others would be able to see which were still available.

Gustav joined us. "I t'ink it would be a goot idea for Vicente and Angie to have the first hut, ya?"

"I agree, Gustav," I said. "Their privacy and comfort are more important and immediate because of the pregnancy. Good idea."

"Which one do you prefer?" Carl asked me, pointing the stick at one square and then the other.

I leaned down and made a small X. "This one—next door to Vicente and Angie."

The couple in question appeared and gazed at the sand sketch, noting that we had marked their location as #1, ours with #2.

"We're going to be neighbors!" I said, and hugged Angie. Carl shook Vicente's hand and congratulated him on his upcoming fatherhood.

With something to look forward to—and to get our minds off the fact that we may never be rescued—the entire group seemed invigorated. The very next day, men and women alike congregated in Town Hall, as we decided to rename the communal building, right after breakfast to begin work on the first hut. Everyone unanimously agreed it should be Vicente and Angie's.

Lacking saws or modern cutting tools, the most backbreaking part of the job was collecting saplings for the walls. We created rudimentary axes by tying sharp-edged stones to wooden handles with tough vines collected from the jungle and selected slim trees. The first few days were the most grueling.

Jasper had disappeared even before work commenced, but no one complained. Even when he was present, he was so disagreeable and lazy that he created more work for everyone else and the atmosphere was downright cheerful without him.

The women had offered to rotate as lookouts, allowing the men uninterrupted time to work on the house. Sheila took the first four-hour stint beginning at six in the morning. Teresa relieved her at ten and Angie took over at two o'clock.

We knocked off work for the day around 5:00 so we could fix dinner and clean up before darkness fell. When the meal was almost ready, I climbed our now well-worn path to the lookout ridge to get Angie and was surprised when I didn't see her waiting for me.

"Angie?" I called. "Angie?" Met with only silence, I walked along the ridge and looked down the side of the mountain. Nothing. The unbroken panoramic view of the ocean was enough to take your breath away—unless you were praying for a ship to appear. I turned and headed back to the landing at the top of the path.

"Angie? Dinner's ready. Where are you?"

The bushes lining the edge of the trail rustled and I stopped, my heart in my throat, expecting to see monkeys peering back at me from the brush. I frantically glanced around for an escape route and saw only up on one side, down on the other. The bushes rustled again and, as I watched, a human hand tentatively reached out from between the leaves and lay still upon the ground.

Is that blood?

Rusty red streaked the back of the hand and crusted the fingernail beds. Horrified, not knowing what I might find and still half expecting to be attacked, I picked up a fist-sized rock and tentatively moved to the bush, holding the rock high. I parted the branches. Angie lay huddled on the ground in the fetal position, nearly naked, her hair matted with blood, dirt, and leaves.

I tossed the rock aside and dropped to my knees. "Angie, Angie-baby, it's me, Laralee."

She whimpered like a savagely kicked dog and my heart broke. I gently touched her arm and she flinched, pulling away as though expecting another brutal attack.

"It's okay," I murmured. "It's Laralee. It's okay, honey, come on out."

I gripped her wrist to help her out of the bushes, but she violently yanked her hand away and scrabbled backwards deeper into the undergrowth, pressing her back hard against the rock wall. A keening sound like I'd never heard from another human being came from deep in her throat.

My gaze slid over her, assessing her injuries. Her left eye was swollen shut, that cheekbone bruised, and her nose had bled and caked with dried blood. Her split and bloody lower lip contrasted sharply with the ugly purple of the jawbone. Her one open eye darted desperate glances everywhere like a cornered animal looking for a way to escape. I knew she didn't recognize me.

What in God's name had happened to her?

"Angie? It's Laralee, honey. I'm not going to hurt you," I soothed. "I'm just going to sit here, okay? Is that alright?"

When I stopped moving, the keening gradually subsided and Angie's body relaxed. The wildness seeped from her eye as I kept up a running monologue, saying whatever came to mind in an effort to connect.

"Look at me, honey. Can you look at me?"

Slowly, Angie raised her head and looked me in the eye. I saw a faint flicker of recognition. "It's Laralee, Angie," I said softly. "It's almost dinner time. Do you want to go see Vicente?" I hoped that speaking of normal things would reduce her fear and encourage her to come out of the bushes. I couldn't leave her here alone—not even to go for help.

I held out my hand, palm up, as non-threatening as possible, hoping she would come to me. After a long moment, she began to crawl in my direction. I waited.

When she reached the bushes, I spread the branches and allowed her to come out on her own, so I wouldn't spook her back into hiding.

As she stood, her shirt and bra hung from one shoulder and she wore only a ripped pair of pink lace panties. Blood streaked her chest and I saw deep, human teeth marks on her breasts before she tried to cover herself.

I had my suspicions about who had attacked her, but I needed to know. Softly, I asked, "Honey, can you tell me who did this?"

Her head whipped around, her body tensed, and that wild look returned. I felt she was about to dive back into the brush.

"It's okay, Angie," I said quickly. "He's gone. I promise he's gone and he's not going to hurt you anymore."

"He's gone? He's gone?" she whimpered, stepping close to me.

I gently wrapped my arms around her and she clung to me, terrified and trembling. "Yes, he's gone." I smoothed her matted hair and made soothing sounds until she quit shaking. "Can you tell me who did this?"

With her face buried in my shoulder, she stammered, "J-J-Jasper." When she uttered his name, she screamed and collapsed at my feet. I sat with her, rocked her, and cried with her, envisioning the animal that had done this.

He will pay!

Chapter 9

WE LIMPED into camp with Angie wearing my blouse. I called to Carl and he quickly removed his shirt and handed it to me.

"Get Gustav," I said quietly, pulling the shirt over my head.

Everyone had gathered in Town Hall to relax before dinner, so Carl asked them to leave as Gustav and I helped Angie lie down. Thankfully, Vicente had gone crabbing with Bruce—I didn't want to have to deal with him just yet.

She held my hand in a vice and wouldn't let me leave, so I motioned for Carl to wait outside.

Gustav took one look at her and stabbed me with his eyes. "Who did t'is?" he hissed.

I mouthed "Jasper."

He shook his head and began to examine her.

"Is my baby alright?" she cried. "Is it alright?"

"Lie still, little one, and let me look at you," Gustav comforted. His experience with skittish animals stood him in good stead as he soothed Angie's fears and calmed her with his soft voice and gentle hands.

Later, she fell asleep, exhausted from the trauma.

Gustav and I exited Town Hall and found the whole group—minus Jasper, of course—waiting anxiously. Vicente and Bruce just that moment returned from the beach.

"What's going on? Are we having a meeting?" Vicente asked.

"Come," I said. "We need to talk." I motioned for Carl to follow in case I needed him.

I led Vicente to a clearing where we could sit and converse in private and related what Angie had told me about the rape. She had fought hard and scratched Jasper's face severely—the source of the blood caked around her nails—before he had pulled his knife and held it to her throat.

Vicente reacted as I expected, and I was glad Carl was there to physically restrain him from going after the attacker.

"No, Vicente!" I said. "Angie needs you with her, not chasing after the animal who did this."

"He needs to pay! He could've killed her...and the baby!" he sobbed.

"Yes, he does need to pay. But not now. Angie needs you." For the second time that day, I held someone in my arms while he wept.

When the sobbing stopped, Vicente wiped his face and stood. "I'll be with Angie." He strode back toward Town Hall looking more mature and resolute than before. There's nothing like a tragedy to force someone to grow up.

For the next two days, Vicente spent every moment with Angie, their bond growing deeper as they learned how to cope with the assault together.

Gustav confided in me that he'd told them he didn't think the baby had been harmed—it was early in the pregnancy and she hadn't suffered any vaginal bleeding. It was her face and breasts that had taken the brunt of the beast's cruelty.

Jasper had ripped Angie's clothes to shreds during the attack and Sheila did her best to stitch them back together with fibers from a vine. Although the clothing looked odd, at least Angie had something to wear.

We worked diligently on the first one-room hut and before long, it took shape. Without heating, air conditioning, wiring or plumbing, the flooring and walls went up quickly. The thatched roof provided an exotic appearance. Using shorter limbs, we created a shutter tied to the saplings above the window openings with sturdy vines that could be swung shut for privacy and would provide a barrier against rain and insects. We even built a door of sorts—also tied at the side—that could be opened in the daytime and closed and tied shut at night. Sometimes the mosquitos could be quite annoying.

Vicente appeared for work one day wearing a sheepish grin. "Angie told me to come work on our house. I think I'm getting on her nerves."

I laughed. "That means she's feeling better. Take it as a good sign." Handing him a length of vine, I said, "Here, help me with this shutter."

That day, we finished their hut and quit work early to go fishing. Guillermo and Sheila had planned another seafood feast to celebrate Angie and Vicente moving into their new pad. Dinner that night was a festive affair and with Angie's bruises fading and her swollen eye nearly back to normal, we could almost forget about the animal that freely roamed the island—except for his conspicuous absence.

The next morning, work commenced on the next house—ours.

And…I needed to talk to Carl.

"Honey, let's take a walk after breakfast. We haven't strolled through the jungle for a while and I'm missing the sound of the birds in the trees."

I could see the glint in his eyes and knew he thought I wanted a tryst with my husband. He'd be surprised.

We walked hand in hand for a while before I stopped and sat on a log. I didn't want to go too far but we needed privacy for the conversation we were about to have. "What do you think of Angie's pregnancy? Will she be able to deliver a healthy child living here on the island?"

"I don't see why not," he said. "Now that we're eating seafood in addition to the fruit and Guillermo's incorporating greens and nuts into our meals, we're probably eating a more balanced diet than if we were back home. She's a healthy young woman and gets plenty of exercise and fresh air. Why?"

"Well," I paused and looked him in the eye. "Angie's not the only one who's pregnant."

It took a minute for the news to sink in. But finally, his eyes grew wide and he stammered, "Are-are you saying that...are you saying we're having a baby, too?"

I nodded, wearing a huge smile. "I didn't want to say anything until I was absolutely sure, but I think I'm about two months along."

"Oh, my God, a baby." Tears formed in Carl's eyes. He wrapped his long arms around me and pulled me close.

Holding him tight, I debated about whether to broach the next subject or not. "You know I love you more than life itself, don't you?"

He leaned back and gazed at me through glimmering eyes. "Yes, as I love you."

I looked down at the fallen leaves at our feet. "And that makes this even more difficult to put into words."

He frowned. "What, Laralee?"

"Do you really want to bring a child into this life? I hate to say it, but we may never be rescued. We may live out the rest of our days here. What kind of life is that?"

He paused for so long that eventually I looked up to see what expression he wore. *Is he angry with me?*

Savage Isle

His handsome, craggy features changed as various emotions assaulted him. I saw his initial joy change to anger, sadness, fear...

Finally, he said, "Laralee, you are my life—no matter where we are. A child is a product of our immense love for each other so regardless of what type of life we're living or where we're living it, a child will be raised with love and encouragement and understanding. We will share with him—or her—our incredible love. Not many people get the chance to experience what we have together." He smiled a smile that lit up the world.

"So, to answer your original question...yes! I do want to have our baby. Here, there, anywhere at all! A child is a wonderful gift—and the only person I would willingly share you with."

It was my turn for tears to overflow. I pulled my husband into my arms and whispered, "You are the most incredible husband a woman could ask for. 'I love you' doesn't seem to say enough."

As it turned out, we did have a lover's tryst in the jungle that morning—a gentle, loving, celebration of life. Afterwards, sated and filled with love for this exceptional man, I lay on our pile of palm fronds staring into his adoring eyes. Happy tears blurred my vision. A nearby rustle forced my gaze from Carl's face and I caught a blurry glimpse of a dark body moving in the brush. A fetid smell wafted through the air.

"Run!" I said.

A puzzled look replaced Carl's doting expression. He obviously hadn't noticed the smell or the rustling in the brush.

"Monkeys!" I hissed. "Move!"

We grabbed our clothing and dashed toward camp. Overhead swishing in the leaves and crackling of limbs indicated the beasts followed us but remained in the trees. We stopped at the edge of camp to compose ourselves and when we entered the clearing, we found a flurry of activity—work had begun on our hut.

We had agreed to remain silent—for now—about the monkeys, but Carl couldn't wait to share our happier news. "Can I have everyone's attention, please?"

Laughter and banging stopped as all eyes turned his way.

Holding my hand and grinning from ear to ear, he said, "I...*we* have an announcement to make. Angie's not the only one who's pregnant."

Cheers, clapping, and whistles erupted from the guys as the women ran to congratulate me. Angie had come to the work site today for the first time since the attack and she wrapped her arms around me in a big hug. She whispered, "Our kids can grow up together. They'll be about the same age." Beaming, she added, "This'll be so much fun!"

I grinned at her exuberance. "It does give us a good reason to finish these huts, doesn't it? Let's get back to work. We can celebrate when the house is done."

Now that we had one hut under our belt, the second went faster. As the celebratory dinner wound down and Carl and I were preparing to move into our new home, he addressed the group.

"Tomorrow we can start the next hut." Waggling his eyebrows suggestively, he asked, "Is anyone else pregnant?" Amidst the laughter, all eyes swiveled toward Sheila and Guillermo.

Blushing a deep red, Sheila said so softly it was hard to hear, "Not yet."

"Well, just to be on the safe side," Carl said, "we'll start on yours next." Then he added, "Next rainy season we'll have to figure out something else to do so not everyone gets pregnant again!"

Guffaws followed us as Carl and I made our way to our new home. Climbing the stairs, I was glad we'd planned all the dwellings to be on stilts about three feet off the ground to make it more difficult for snakes and other critters to get in. It would also help during the rainy season when water often lay in puddles or created rivulets in low spots. With the buildings elevated, they'd stay drier.

Earlier, we had hauled palm fronds in to create a comfortable bed and it looked inviting. This was the first night since the wreck that we weren't sleeping in a dorm and we made the most of our newfound privacy.

Later, I broached the subject we'd been avoiding since earlier that day, although I kept my voice low. "The monkeys are getting bolder. They seem to have greatly reduced the prey population on the island and I'm afraid we may be next."

Carl was silent for so long I thought perhaps he'd fallen asleep. Finally, in a voice filled with sadness and fear, he said, "I think you may be right."

He pulled me close, holding me so tight I could barely breathe, and whispered, "I have to figure out a way to keep you and the baby safe."

***

Several weeks later, due to everyone's concerted efforts, we had completed huts for Vicente and Angie, Carl and myself, Guillermo and Sheila, and Gustav and Teresa. Over breakfast, Carl posed an awkward question to Bruce and Caroline.

"Do you each want separate quarters?"

Caroline blushed and glanced at Bruce. "It seems silly to build two more huts," she said. "And I'd feel safer not being alone at night. What if we had one hut with separate rooms?"

Bruce rolled his eyes. "Works for me. It's not like we're going to be *living* there, just sleeping."

"Alright," Carl said. "We'll make number five a little bigger and put a dividing wall down the center. Both rooms will be the same size so you two can decide who gets which one."

Before long, we had an entire row of thatched-roof, stilted huts meandering along the shore between the sand and the edge of the tree line. We were close, so everyone felt secure, but separated enough for nighttime privacy. Town Hall became our communal dining room, meeting place, and general lounging area.

With the huts finished, we decided to erect a somewhat portable bathroom. For obvious reasons, we didn't want it too far from our living area but neither did we want it too close. Again, using vines, we strapped saplings together to create wall panels, lashing them together at the corners to form a temporary building like the public restrooms at a typical beach—open-air yet with a semblance of privacy. We dug holes in the ground that could be filled in when we deemed it time to relocate, and we could simply pick up the walls and move them to another spot. We fashioned toilets out of rock to make life a bit easier—however, as much as we might wish for all the modern conveniences, flushing was still out of the question.

Once the work was completed, Angie and I compared our baby-bumps as we strolled along the beach. I had never heard nor smelled the monkeys near the shore so felt safer than if we'd opted to take a walk in the trees.

Neither of us had suffered major morning sickness, but I was longing for—no, *craving*—chocolate. I think I would've gnawed the bark off a tree if someone had told me there was chocolate inside.

"Look." Angie pointed. "A bottle."

We scurried to the surf line and she plucked the container jutting bottom-up from the sand. Unbroken, it looked like a soda bottle, but all markings had been erased by the eroding action of water and sand. No telling how long it had been in the ocean.

Suddenly, I shouted, "Glass! It's glass!"

I startled Angie so badly she nearly dropped the bottle. "Yes, it is, Laralee. What's the big deal?"

"We can use it to start a fire!" I grabbed it out of her hand and waved it in the air. Overjoyed, I yelled, "We can cook *fooooood!*"

The look on her face would've won a Kodak 'once-in-a-lifetime moment' contest. I could tell exactly when she connected the dots.

"Oh, my God," she yelled. "You're right!"

We whirled and ran back to the village as fast as two clumsily pregnant women could run.

Carl leapt to his feet and grabbed a fist-sized rock. Running past, he growled, "What? What is it?"

Still on a high about our find, I couldn't figure out where he was going. Then I realized he thought something was chasing us and was going to save us with his rock. Stifling a laugh, I went to him and said, "I love you for wanting to protect us, but we're just excited. Look!"

I held up the bottle. "It washed up on shore."

Our simultaneous exclamations overlapped. I said, "We can use it to start a fire" and he said, "A vessel for water." I'm sure I looked as confused as I felt.

"For water?" I asked. "No! We can amplify the heat from the sun and start fires for cooking. It's better than I expected it to be, but we won't have to eat raw fish anymore." Then another thought crossed my mind. "Maybe we can even catch a rabbit and have *meat* for dinner!" My mouth watered.

Furrows formed between Carl's brows. I knew that look. He was on to something.

"What? What are you thinking?" I asked.

"Maybe we can do both."

"Both what?"

"Carry water *and* start a fire."

"Alright," I said. "Now you've lost me."

"Take off your diamond ring."

Puzzled, I pulled my engagement ring off. We had vowed to never remove our rings, so I knew he must have a good reason for asking.

"Diamond cuts glass. I'm going to try and cut the neck off the bottle and we can use the bottom for a cup and the top to start a fire."

I giggled. "I married a genius."

"You can call me a genius if it works," he said.

Laying the bottle flat on the sand, he held the ring tightly between his thumb and first finger. He pressed the edge of the diamond against the glass and slowly spun the bottle. I could hear the stone grating against the glass and prayed it would score deeply enough to enable us to break it.

When the cut completely encircled the bottle's neck, Carl examined it closely and handed the ring back.

He tapped the score line sharply on the corner of a rock. Nothing. He tapped it again, harder. The neck split in two and fell off, leaving the cup-shaped bottom intact.

"Yes!" he yelled.

I gave him a smacking kiss right on the lips. "My genius."

He grinned and not-so-humbly said, "Okay, maybe I am." He then grabbed me, pulled me close, and claimed my lips in a long, sensuous kiss. "Now, *that's* a reward!"

I giggled when he reached for me again and playfully slapped at his hands. "Go on, Genius, finish the job."

Savage Isle

Taking the bottom part of the bottle, he rubbed the razor-sharp, top edges on a flat rock littered with sand. It would have to be smooth if we were to drink from it. After a few minutes, he ran his thumb over the once-sharp lip and pronounced it safe.

He then turned his attention to the two neck parts. "We can use this narrow sliver as a knife."

"When we're done here, I'll go find a vine to wrap around one end," I offered. "Sand the one end like you did the cup. The other end can be the cutting edge."

"No wonder we make such a great pair," he said, winking at me. Then he examined the last part. "This wider portion should work as a fire-starter." He grinned up at Angie and me. "You two are the geniuses. Life just got a little bit easier."

"And tastier," I added. "I'll go get the vine for the knife. Then we're going fishing!"

Bruce and Guillermo had appointed themselves our fishermen so when they heard we had a potential fire-starter, they grabbed their spears. Luck smiled on us that day. A medium-sized ray had become trapped in a pool and soon fell prey to the men's increasingly skillful thrusts.

While the guys were fishing, the rest of us caught crabs on the beach. I, for one, envisioned a *cooked* seafood buffet. *Now, if only we had a little butter, salt, and pepper...*

As Guillermo cleaned the day's catch, Carl scrubbed the glass shard until it sparkled and then set it on two rocks with dry grass and bits of bark beneath. I watched the entire process carefully and sat on a nearby rock to document approximately how long before the heat of the tropical sun sparked the tinder into flame.

At first, nothing. My heart sank as I wondered if this would work, after all. Then, a tiny piece of grass shriveled. A whisper of smoke wafted upward. Just as a bright yellow spot appeared at the base of the smoke, a flame licked at the handful of grass and the whole thing caught.

"It worked! It worked!" I yelled. "We have fire!" Gently tossing on more bits of bark and small twigs, I coaxed the tiny flames into a cooking-sized blaze. We arranged rocks along the edges to contain it and before long, Guillermo placed a flat rock containing 'ray steaks' over the cooking pit. Once it heated up and the fish began to sizzle, he dropped crabs in between the fish. The smell of cooking food made my mouth water. Nothing had *ever* smelled so delicious!

Chapter 10

I FELT LIKE the first cave man that had discovered fire. It changed our lives—most certainly, our diet—but at least we didn't need the heat to keep warm during long, frozen winters.

We began trapping rabbits and squirrels for their meat. Occasionally the men would hunt a wild pig, but they were quick, weren't averse to charging human attackers, and could be extremely dangerous. We were quite conscious of the fact that we had no first aid kit. Even a slight injury could prove fatal without soap to thoroughly clean it, antibiotics to fight infection, or the ability to set and cast broken bones. Gustav was a great asset, but he was no miracle-worker. As a result, pig-hunting expeditions were few and far between.

One day when Bruce and Vicente went to check on the rabbit snares, they returned with two rabbits plus potatoes, carrots, and onions.

"Where did you find those?" I cried, elated.

"I tripped over something and found out it was a potato," Vicente said. "It looked like we'd found an old garden, so we collected as many vegetables as we could carry."

"You have to show me where it is. We can cultivate the veggies and have some for dinner whenever we want." I felt like I'd died and gone to heaven. If we had to stay here indefinitely, at least we could eat more than the same old things all the time.

After that, we pulled the weeds trying to choke the life out of the garden and propagated more plants so we'd never run out. We became hunters and gatherers, fishermen and farmers.

We also fortified our huts. Bruce and Vicente had encountered a small band of the dark, smelly monkeys on their way back from the vegetable garden and everyone said they had noticed numerous monkeys in the trees nearby much more often.

Inside shutters in each hut that could be braced with two horizontal saplings made our quarters more secure. This innovative 'lock' would prevent anyone, or anything, from forcing its way in through the windows. We did the same with the doors.

As my fear for our safety increased, Angie and I grew large with child and spent a lot of time together. In addition to sharing impending motherhood, the assault had bonded us in a way no one else understood. I had seen her at her very worst—at the edge of insanity—and had coaxed her back from the brink of that black abyss. I knew how much she wanted Jasper dead.

That became a very real issue one day about six months after the rape. Vicente approached Carl and me after lunch—the others had wandered off and we'd stayed in Town Hall to relax and talk. We waited patiently as he paced back and forth. Finally, he stopped. In a low and deadly serious voice, he said, "We have to do something about Jasper."

"What did you have in mind?" Carl asked.

I held my breath. *This could be bad.*

"I don't know." He paced again. "Angie never sleeps through the night. She has nightmares and wakes up screaming—I'm sure you've heard her."

Living right next door, we were aware of her bad dreams and sleeplessness. Everyone could hear her screams. I nodded.

"It can't be good for the baby," he continued. "And if she does manage to get to sleep, the slightest sound jolts her awake. Then she leans against the wall, trembling, for the rest of the night. I think she expects him to come back and attack her again."

He turned to face us. "We *have* to do something. She has dark circles under her eyes and bursts into tears for no reason. She's making *me* a nervous wreck."

Carl patted the rock beside him. "Sit for a minute."

Vicente took a seat and hung his head. The silence grew and became so loud I was surprised I heard his next comment.

"He needs to die."

Carl and I shared a look before Vicente glanced up. "If we were back home and he raped her, he'd be arrested, have a trial, and go to jail for as many years as they could legally lock him up." He stood and resumed pacing.

"You saw what that animal did to her!" He stopped moving and glared at me.

"It took *weeks* before I could even touch her, before I could hold her. She needed me desperately, but because I'm a *man* she couldn't stand to have me near her."

He swiped angrily at a tear on his cheek.

"Even now, I have to be gentle with her and can never restrain her in any way. If she turns over in the night and my arm's around her, she whimpers and pulls away."

Pausing, he took a deep breath and looked out toward the sea. When he spoke again, the icy determination in his voice frightened me.

"He lost his rights as a human being the day he acted like a savage animal and forced himself on her. If no one else will help me, I'll go after him myself."

I rose and went to stand in front of him. Looking up into a face seemingly chiseled from granite, I put my hands on his arms. "Vicente, please don't do anything until we have a chance to talk to the rest of the group. Can you promise me that?"

His dark eyes bored into mine. "Yes. I promise. Just don't take too long." He turned on his heel and strode away.

The emotional young man who had begged to go home after the monkeys ripped off his ear was nowhere in sight. In his stead walked a resolute man determined to get justice for the woman he loved. My heart swelled with pride for the man he had become and then quaked with fear at what the future might hold.

Later that day, when everyone had gathered at Town Hall prior to the evening meal, Carl called a meeting.

"You all know that Jasper is the one who attacked Angie," he began.

Heads nodded. Murmuring started, then stopped.

"Vicente came to me today with a request on Angie's behalf. He made a good point, but I'm not quite sure how to proceed. At home, Jasper would have been arrested, brought to trial, and sentenced for his brutal crime. Here, unless *we* do something, he walks away scot free. And that is unacceptable!"

Murmuring grew to a soft roar. Carl let them rile each other up, watching the level of anger and desire for revenge rise.

"Should we let him get away with it?" he asked.

"No!"

"Hell, no!"

"He deserves to hang!"

Amid the ruckus, Vicente walked to the front and held up his hands for silence. His new maturity now commanded respect. A hush fell over the group.

"Most of you know me…and know I'm not a violent man. If the attack had been on me, I'd have come to terms with it and gone on with my life." He paused and hung his head.

When he raised his eyes to the group once again, fire seemed to rage in his soul. "But the assault was on one of the kindest, sweetest women on the face of this earth. She did not deserve what happened to her, but she *does* deserve justice!"

His voice rose and the fire all but leapt from his eyes. "I *will* find Jasper. And I *will* deliver justice for Angie—making this island a safer place for all of us. I'd welcome your help."

Vicente turned and walked away as the room erupted into chaos.

Once again, Carl stood and raised his hands for silence. It took a little longer, but eventually the room went quiet.

"You know what Vicente is proposing, right?"

"An eye for an eye!" Bruce yelled.

Gustav stood. I had no idea what to expect from him.

"I am not a violent man eit'er, but if a dog is rabid, you put it down to prevent more harm coming to ot'ers. T'is, I feel, is t'e same. He must be put down to prevent more harm. I will help."

He took his seat and Teresa laced her fingers through his.

Guillermo rose. "If we don't help Vicente take down this vicious animal, who will he attack next? It could be Sheila—and I couldn't live with myself if that happened and I'd done nothin' to prevent it. I'm in."

Gazing around the room, I realized we were talking about murdering a man—and the scariest part of the whole discussion was that the rationale made sense. *Can we really do this?*

Before I could stop myself, I stood and walked to the fore. "No one knows better than I what Jasper did to Angie.

None of you saw the utter terror in her eyes; heard the whimpering, beaten-dog sounds coming from her lips. None of you coaxed her out of the bushes, nearly naked, bleeding and incoherent." I waited a beat to let it sink in.

"But we're talking about murdering a man..." The babble began and I held up my hands. "Please, let me finish." I waited for the quiet.

"Does Jasper deserve to be punished for what he did? Absolutely. Should we turn the other cheek and hope he doesn't attack anyone else? No, probably not. But do we have the right to be judge, jury, and executioner? If we take his life, are we really any better than he is just because we agreed—as a group—to do it?"

I sat down and listened to the raucous voices around me. Then suddenly, everything went still. When I looked up, I saw that Angie had taken the spot I'd just vacated.

She inhaled deeply, then let the air out. "There's something I haven't told you." Looking at me, she mouthed, "I'm sorry," and wiped at a tear.

"Up on the ridge that day, with his knife at my throat, his rutting body on top of mine, Jasper told me he *would* come back. He wanted me to know that he'll be watching and will know when I have my child. And if it's a girl, he'll take me and then he'll take her, too. In his sick and twisted mind, he believes he owns me and he'll never let me go." Tears streamed down her face as she held her baby-belly with both hands.

"Please! You *have* to stop him. If not for me, then for her." She looked down at her stomach. "I know it's a girl. And he. *Cannot*. Touch her."

As though it had taken all the strength she possessed to say what she'd said, Angie collapsed. Standing directly behind her, Carl caught her before she hit the ground, and carried her to the house. Gustav followed.

I sat with her during the examination in case she regained consciousness. Her utter stillness scared me.

"She is exhausted," Gustav said, "and needs t'e sleep. She and t'e baby would do best if we let her rest. T'e stress of knowing what t'at animal plans to do has taken a toll. We must stop him."

In light of the new information, my feelings had changed. In my mind, he was no longer a man who had committed a terrible mistake by giving in to his lust. He was a willing predator lying in wait for the chance to reclaim his last victim—and her child. I had no doubt he would strike again, and Angie would never be safe as long as Jasper walked the earth. *I'm in.*

I took Vicente food as he sat beside her sleeping form. "This is the first deep sleep she's had in months," he said. The granite of his face softened as he gazed at her. "Do you know what happened? Why she collapsed?"

There was no point in not telling him when everyone else knew, but I was afraid of what he might do.

"You said she seems convinced Jasper will come back and attack her again."

"Yes, for some reason she is."

I held him with my eyes. "That's because he told her he would."

"What?" he exclaimed sharply. "She never told me that."

"She didn't tell anyone."

"Then how…?"

"After you left today, I spoke out against going after Jasper."

He started to argue and I put my hand on his arm. "Hear me out, okay?"

He nodded, a small pulse at his jawline pounding a strong, dangerous rhythm.

"You had everyone all riled up and ready to lynch the man. I wasn't comfortable being judge, jury, and executioner and suggested that we'd be as bad as he is if we took matters into our own hands. It's not up to us to make that decision.

"Then Angie confronted the group and told us what he'd said. Afterwards, she collapsed." When I paused, Vicente stared at me, hard.

"What did that animal say to her?" he asked through clenched teeth.

I let my breath out in a whoosh. "He said he owns her. That he'll be watching and will know when she has the baby." I paused again.

"And?"

"He said he'll come back for her…and if the child is a girl, he'll take her, too."

Vicente jumped up and paced furiously back and forth across the room, his face flushed and contorted with anger. His hands coiled into rock-solid fists. When he finally stopped in front of me, he said, "I will not let him lay a hand on Angie or my daughter, with or without your help."

I nodded. "After hearing what he said to her, I couldn't ignore the fact that the man is a vicious animal and deserves to be treated like one. I'll not judge you for protecting your family."

The next morning, all ten of us converged in Town Hall with only one thing on our minds. Jasper.

After her first good night's sleep in many months, even Angie appeared stronger, invigorated, and anxious to be a part of whatever was about to transpire.

Due to her startling confession the previous day, Carl and I had agreed we shouldn't speak loudly enough for Jasper to overhear if he was, indeed, nearby and watching. Carl split the assemblage into two small groups and visited them each individually with the same low-voiced message.

"Our mission is to find out where Jasper lives, where he hangs out, where he sleeps, where he loiters to watch Angie. We get a feel for his life, his habits, what he does, and where he goes. If he falls into our lap, we take him, but today is mainly about collecting information. He's been watching us for months—now it's our turn."

Pinning Vicente with a hard stare, he added, "No one does anything in the heat of the moment, understand?" He waited until Vicente nodded and then looked over the rest of the group.

Under cover of Town Hall, the men learned hand signals so they could communicate silently. While they practiced, the rest of us chatted about breakfast and babies—and planned.

Angie, Caroline, Sheila, Teresa, and I would play decoy, but no one would venture out alone, even to the bathroom. We'd be discreetly armed with hand-carved, wooden knives tucked into our clothing so they wouldn't be easily seen. One man would accompany us, armed, ostensibly to protect us from the monkeys.

All men would each carry a heavy club and tuck billy-clubs and short, pointed spears into a vine tied around their waists. In addition, three of the five would carry their pocketknives. They'd be as armed as they could be. The good news was, we knew Jasper didn't have access to more advanced weapons, either, and our men outnumbered him five-to-one.

The day we carried out our plan, to divert Jasper's attention from Town Hall, we women collected fruit and headed to the beach. Bruce came with us, complaining, as usual, about having to babysit—it was a perfect role for him.

As we left, I called, "You guys work on that leak in the roof today. We don't want to get wet during dinner the next time it rains."

Nervous due to more than just the thought of Jasper watching, we followed a well-traveled path to a spot farthest from the village knowing he should prefer watching us over the men. Laughing, joking, and trying to appear unconcerned, we took our time and stopped often to admire the wildflowers growing alongside the trail. Bruce brought up the rear, mostly so we wouldn't have to listen to his complaints.

Without being obvious about it, Angie stayed in the middle of the pack, never lagging or roaming ahead. We wanted Jasper to follow, but not have an opportunity to separate her from the group. At the beach, we relaxed a little, knowing the monkeys wouldn't be here, strolled up and down the shoreline collecting shells, giggled, and tried to be entertaining enough that Jasper wouldn't get bored and leave. Bruce found a big rock to lean on and dozed.

"Do you feel like catching crabs for dinner?" I asked.

Angie moaned. "Only if someone with a waistline smaller than a Beluga whale picks them up. I'll point 'em out."

Teresa, Caroline, and Sheila happily obliged, darting here and there to capture the hapless crustaceans. We'd brought a T-shirt to use as a holding tank.

Pausing and shading her eyes with her hand, Angie faced the sea. She whispered, "He's here. I can feel his filthy eyes on me."

"You're doing fine, Angie," I said reassuringly. "Let him look. If he's here with us, the men have a better chance of finding his lair. If he charges us, he'll be met by five, armed Mama Bears—and Bruce, if he can get up from the sand fast enough. And we know Jasper's a coward at heart."

Savage Isle

As we wandered farther up the shore, I kept one eye on the water, fascinated by the sharks that patrolled the shallows and noticed several fins a short distance out. Carl had mentioned trying to swim to the wreck to recover items we could use, but I had vehemently resisted. I'd do without *things* before I would do without my husband.

A gleam in the sand caught my attention and I waddled over to find another bottle, although this one wasn't intact. It did, however, have a useable bottom if Carl could sand the jagged edges off. *Another cup.*

The sun slowly assumed a late afternoon angle. "Are you gals ready to head home? My back hurts," I said.

"My feet hurt," Angie moaned.

"See what you have to look forward to, Sheila? Someday you'll get to enjoy all the perks of pregnancy." We forced a laugh and turned toward the trail, Bruce again bringing up the rear, carrying the T-shirt containing the crabs. This time, we didn't stop along the way, anxious to return to the relative safety of Town Hall and find out how the recon mission had gone.

I heard no twigs cracking on the trail behind us, but the rustling in the overhead canopy indicated we weren't alone and I was glad that Bruce was along despite his griping.

As we entered the three-sided dwelling, Carl yelled, "I hope you ladies had a nice time at the beach while we worked our asses off fixing your ceiling. It's not going to leak again any time soon."

We made a fuss over the great (pretend) job they had done and Bruce held up the bag of crabs.

"I guess that was a pretty good trade-off, after all," Vicente said. "You bring home dinner and all we have to do is clean it, cook it, and eat it."

"Next time they want to go to the beach, someone else can babysit," Bruce said. "I've had my turn."

"We'll go collect some salad greens," Guillermo said, rolling his eyes. "Come on, Sheila."

They dashed away as the rest of us sank gratefully onto the nearest seats.

Carl set up the fire-starter and it reminded me of the partial bottle I'd found that day.

"Look here!" I held it up, carefully keeping my fingers away from the jagged edge.

"Aha! Another cup. At this rate," Carl said, taking it gingerly from my hand, "we might someday have a matched service for four."

Guillermo and Sheila returned, each with an armload of greens. They had stopped at the creek to wash them off and proceeded to cut carrots and onions to go into the salad. As they chopped, I softly asked Carl how the mission had gone.

"We found his camp and where he sleeps," he whispered. "It's not far from here. Do you know whether he followed you to the beach?"

"I think so," I said. "At one point, Angie said she could feel his eyes on her. And I heard a couple twigs snap in the brush on our way there. I don't think he bothered following us home, though."

"Sending you ladies out as decoys goes against everything I believe in. We're supposed to be protecting you, not using you as bait. Even with Bruce along, it just doesn't seem right." Carl shook his head. "I don't like this at all. One man isn't going to be able to protect all of you from the monkeys."

"Honey, desperate times call for desperate measures. We never felt like we were in danger and had our knives tucked into our clothes close at hand. Jasper would've been in for one helluva surprise had he charged us. The monkeys, too, for that matter."

"I still don't like it."

"What if we wait a week or so and set a trap?" I asked.

"What kind of trap?" he scowled. "It had better not include using you as bait."

"As a group—all of us—we can wander to the beach sometime within the next few days and check what location would be best for a trap. Then, a few days after that, us girls can do what we did today and lure Jasper there. He won't be expecting anything and will be engrossed in watching us. You guys sneak up on him and spring the trap."

"I wish we could come up with some other way to lure him there without putting you ladies at risk," Carl muttered.

"We'll all feel safer with Jasper out of commission and we're willing to do our part. There's safety in numbers and if we stick together, you ought to be able to take him down before he hurts anyone else."

"I'll reserve judgment on the plan until we visit the beach and see what we have to work with," Carl said. "If it's not perfect and foolproof, I'm not going to put you at risk." He shook his head and murmured, "It's like sending you into the lion's den. I don't like it—not one bit."

Chapter 11

SEVERAL DAYS LATER, we packed a picnic lunch of leftover fish and fruit and headed to the beach. Laughing, I said, "So we're taking a vacation, huh? A vacation from what?"

"From the honey-do lists!" Carl answered. "You wouldn't think the list would be very long here, but I swear you women come up with something new every day."

As before, Angie stayed near the center of the pack and she and I purposely set a slow pace, allowing the men ample time to survey the surroundings. When we reached a nice area, we pretended to settle in as the guys scouted its potential. Bruce objected and wanted to move on, citing its lack of adequate fishing pools.

We grumbled, collected our things, and proceeded farther up the shoreline. Here, Teresa objected due to the large number of rocks—she couldn't find a comfortable place to rest.

Our scripted objections should've sounded quite plausible to Jasper, if he was watching.

Finally, Carl stopped. Sounding exasperated, he asked, "Alright, does anyone have any objections to *this* beach?" That was our prearranged signal that he liked the location and its potential for setting a trap.

We gazed around and shook our heads. The guys roamed up and down the shore checking the fishing pools while we settled into an area suitable for lunch. Chatting amongst ourselves, each woman kept a close eye on her man—and a hand close to her knife.

"We're going to scout the jungle for fresh water," Carl called. "We'll be back shortly."

That meant they were going to see if the area offered enough places for the men to conceal themselves while waiting to trap Jasper. My heart pounded as our men filed into the jungle. I felt exposed, sitting there waiting for something to happen.

"Relax, Laralee," Teresa said softly, trying to lighten the mood. "You look like you're waiting for a bomb to explode. I don't think anything will happen while the men are nearby." She whispered, "Smile."

I realized she was probably right and forced a smile as requested. Jasper was a coward and wouldn't want to risk being confronted by the men. He'd wait until we were women alone and defenseless—or so it would appear—before making his move. And he'd told Angie he'd watch until she'd given birth, so he'd know if she had a little girl. I made myself relax.

"I feel like a beached whale," I joked. "I hope no one tries to shove me back out to sea."

Angie giggled. "I know exactly what you mean. I'm glad the sand is pretty level. If it sloped, a breeze would get me rolling like those lightweight beach balls and I'd never stop 'til I reached the bottom!"

We giggled, each of us picturing Angie rolling and bouncing along the beach.

Finally, the men returned and we served lunch. Carl looked grim and I didn't know if that was a good sign or not. I resigned myself to waiting until we had an opportunity to talk.

"Did you find a stream nearby?" I asked instead.

"Yes," he said, "it's not far. This is a perfect spot."

I felt he was telling me this was a good location for a trap and I wanted him to know I understood. "Great. We like it, too." I smiled and handed him a ray steak. "After lunch, we can go fishing in that big pool Vicente found earlier."

Later, we trudged home with the catch-of-the-day, a T-shirt full of crabs, and a plan.

Tangled together in our bed of palm fronds that night, the windows and door shuttered and secure, Carl shared his thoughts with me.

"That beach location is perfect. The jungle has a lot of large trees where the men can hide and there's one thick stand of trees and brush that could easily conceal two men. The rushing stream will provide enough background noise to mask any sounds we might make. It's as good a spot as we're going to find."

"Okay, the next question is when do you want to do this?" I asked. "I think sooner rather than later."

"Why sooner? You and Angie are both about ready to pop. How would you defend yourselves if Jasper attacked? Wouldn't it be better to wait?"

"If we wait, we'll have two infants in our midst. Angie and I would be more focused on protecting the children than anything else."

He sighed deeply. "I guess there's no really good time to do this awful thing, is there?"

Although I didn't speak, I knew he felt my head move back and forth on his shoulder.

After a prolonged silence, I changed the subject. "I wonder what happened to James and Julie. If they survived the wreck, she would've had her baby by now. I hope they're okay."

"Yeah," he said. "I wonder if it was a boy or a girl. And how very smart it is."

Another silence filled the night.

"And thinking about James and Julie makes me think about those awful monkeys." I shuddered, recalling their stench and appetite for flesh. "We know some of them survived and they surely adapted well to life on this island. With lots of food and no predators more ferocious than they are, they must be reproducing, too."

The thought of the monkeys passing their vicious, meat-eating proclivities on to their offspring filled me with dread. "You know, eventually the smaller, easier prey will be gone. I've already noticed a decrease in the number of rabbits, squirrels, birds…even the pigs don't seem as numerous."

"Stop worrying, Laralee. We know they're out there, we're armed and alert, and so far, they haven't attacked. Go to sleep."

I sighed and nestled against my warm, wise husband. "You're right. I'm not going to worry about it any more tonight. I love you."

He squeezed me and brushed his hand lightly over my large belly. "I love you, too, Laralee," he whispered in the dark. "…light of my life, mother of my child. I couldn't survive without you."

***

Several days later, our entire village congregated in Town Hall to decide when we'd set the trap for Jasper. If we were going to do this, we needed to act soon since, according to Angie's and my calculations, we were due to give birth within weeks of each other—both of us in only about five weeks.

Breaking everyone into three smaller groups, Carl went from one to the next with the same message—it was imperative that Jasper not overhear what was said if he was lurking nearby.

"We need a bright, sunny day so the women can go to the beach, leaving the men behind to work on the honey-do list. We'll plan on one week from today to give us additional time to practice and hone our knives—if it's overcast, we'll go the next clear day. Be prepared. Sharpen your knives and spears and be sure your pocketknife is extra sharp. If you have any questions, come to me individually so it's not obvious that we're planning something."

The men secretly practiced their hand signals in Town Hall each afternoon until they came naturally and the night before our scheduled mission, there was little red in the sunset. The old saying, "Red sky at night, sailors' delight" sent us to bed with trepidation.

Sure enough, morning dawned overcast, gloomy, and threatening rain. We waited two more days for the cold front to pass and, finally, a morning dawned bright and clear. As scripted, we teased the men about our day at the beach while they were to stay behind and work on various projects around the houses. "If you get all the work done today," I yelled to Carl as we waddled up the trail, "you boys can go fishing or hunting later in the week."

"Yeah, yeah, yeah," he grumbled theatrically.

"Bring back a truckload of crabs," Vicente called. "We're going to work up a big appetite."

We giggled and trudged ahead, putting on a good show for Jasper and this time, Guillermo accompanied us, bringing up the rear. He complained a lot less than Bruce had.

Nearly to the beach, Angie and I called for a rest. Neither of us had any stamina but carrying a huge load around your middle would cause anyone to pump the brakes.

Lowering myself onto a fallen log, I flexed my toes. My feet and ankles resembled overstuffed sausages, the skin stretched taut over aching joints. I'd be glad when this whole pregnancy thing was over and done with. I couldn't wait to hold my bouncing bundle of joy in my arms instead of out in front. God, my back ached.

Angie carefully placed her butt on the log next to me, helping with the weight distribution by holding onto a sturdy branch.

"Ahhh…that feels good. My feet hurt."

"Mine, too," I muttered. "I may just have to stand in the surf for a few minutes—the water will take some of the swelling down."

Teresa, Sheila, and Caroline lined up in front of us, almost close enough to touch, adhering to the rules about not leaving us alone. Guillermo stood nearby, alert. Sheila started to say something and then choked. Her eyes went wide as she stared past us into the trees.

"What? What is it?" In my enlarged state, I couldn't turn around or get up off the log. My heart thundered as I tried to imagine what was behind us. *Monkeys?*

Her face lost all color and I thought she was going to pass out.

Teresa and Caroline caught Sheila as she swayed and became mute statues, as well. Guillermo pushed forward to wrap his arms around her, all of his attention focused on her pale face. When he raised his eyes to the sight that had shocked everyone, his eyes, too, grew wide, his mouth in a grim, taut line.

I tried to shove myself upright, nearly falling backwards in the process. Angie grabbed the branch and hauled herself to her feet, offering me a helping hand. As quickly as I could, I spun, brandishing my knife, to see what had had such an effect on my friends.

At the edge of a small clearing ten feet away, Jasper hung upside down in a tree, facing us with a look of abject horror in his wide-open, unseeing eyes. He'd been impaled on a branch about five feet off the ground and eviscerated. Many of his internal organs now lay on the ground beneath his dangling body, swimming in a huge, red puddle that had not yet begun to dry.

Angie turned away and heaved into the bushes. I swallowed hard to keep from joining her.

"I'll go get the guys. Stay here," Guillermo said and turned to Sheila. "Will you be okay?"

"Yes. Go."

He spun on his heel and dashed back the way we'd come.

After the initial shock, I studied the scene. From this distance I couldn't be certain, but it looked as though he'd suffered a horrible beating. Bruises purpled his face and both legs hung at odd angles, obviously broken. One arm seemed twisted unnaturally far and many fingers pointed in directions they shouldn't have. Someone—or some*thing*—incredibly strong had taken Jasper's life, relieving us of the odious responsibility. On one hand, it was a great relief to have Jasper out of the way without having had to do anything morally repugnant. On the other, *do we now have an even more dangerous adversary to deal with?*

My thoughts shifted to the ugly monkeys. *Did they do this? But if they had, wouldn't they have eaten him?*

Perhaps the orangutans had protected us. But if they were nearby, I would think they'd have contacted us.

As a group, we backed away from the scene and waited silently for the men to arrive. We had no words to describe the horror and I, for one, concentrated on keeping my breakfast down.

Before long, the men arrived. Carl grabbed me in a bear hug and turned me away from the grisly sight. Vicente, Gustav, and Guillermo held their women, too. All murmured endearments. Bruce led Caroline away and I overheard his concerned questions.

"Are you alright? Do you want to sit down?"

"I'm fine," she answered. "No, I don't want to sit."

Although not a couple, they seemed to have developed a friendship since becoming roommates and his attentive consideration for her warmed my heart. Perhaps the arrogant Boy Scout was growing up.

Once convinced the women were alright, Carl and the others cautiously approached the scene of the crime. My husband looked at the ground, searching. For evidence? Footprints?

Gustav studied the body, a frown wrinkling his forehead, his lips compressed in a straight line.

I couldn't stand being on the sidelines. Shuffling to Gustav's side, I asked, "What do you think did this?"

He glanced at me, then slid his eyes quickly back to the still form hanging from the tree. "I would guess not a man. Perhaps an orangutan."

"Not the vicious monkeys?"

"T'ey are strong, ya, but not tall enough to impale him on t'is branch. It would have to be a larger animal. And t'e monkeys would eat him. I t'ink it was a 'tan."

My emotions battling for dominance within me, I felt angry, disappointed, proud that the 'tans would protect us, happy to think at least one was still alive, and deeply hurt that he/she hadn't reached out to us.

"If it was James or Julie, why wouldn't they have contacted us?" Tears threatened to overflow and I angrily wiped them away.

"T'ey would be scared, too. T'ey have lived free here and would not want to be boxed up again. But t'ey still care and want to protect us. T'at is my guess."

We stood in silence, each of us deep in thought.

Carl walked up and held out his hand. "Look what I found in the blood." Between his thumb and forefinger, he pinched a long, orange-red hair. It was hard to be sure, but it looked like James' coloring.

This time there was no holding back the tears. "It's James! He's alive." I threw my arms around Carl and sobbed with happiness and hysteria. In between catchy breaths, I said, "If only we knew whether Julie survived. And if she has a healthy baby."

According to the crime scene, it seemed that James had ambushed Jasper as he lay in wait for us to pass by the clearing on our way to the beach. And if James had been keeping an eye on us, he would've known that the man was dangerous. He'd taken matters into his own hands and meted out justice in its truest form.

We dug a grave and buried the mutilated body without a eulogy or kind words. Jasper's life had not earned him either.

Relieved to be rid of him, I still felt sad that a life had to end in such a way, but dinner reflected little melancholy. Angie, especially, seemed freed of the weight she had carried on her shoulders for the past months. That very night she went into labor and with the help of our entire village, delivered a healthy, beautiful child. Despite her certainty that she was having a girl, they named their son Roberto.

Chapter 12

WITH THE ARRIVAL of Vicente and Angie's little boy, I knew my time was near, as well. The baby dropped and I carried him low in my belly. I could feel he was anxious to make his entrance into the world.

A week later, large and awkward, I tripped coming down the steps from the hut and landed hard on my backside. Something inside me ripped and I screamed in pain. Before Carl could help me to my feet, I felt the wetness and knew it was time.

"Get Gustav. The baby's coming," I said, pushing Carl's hands away.

"I'll help you up first."

"No! Leave me here. Get Gustav. Hurry!" The pain seemed wrong and I didn't want to move and make things worse. Then I saw the blood mingled with the water and said a prayer for God to save my baby.

Carl and Gustav dashed to my side, the rest of the village right behind them. The men made a stretcher by locking hands and carried me back inside. Teresa volunteered to boil water and Gustav sent everyone but Carl outside as he examined me.

I could tell by his face he was worried. "What is it, Gustav? What's wrong?" I asked.

"T'is blood. It is not goot."

"When I fell, I landed hard and felt a sharp pain inside—like something ripped."

"Ya. We must get t'e baby out right away."

Silent until now, Carl said, "How can we get the baby out? Laralee just went into labor."

"T'e fall tore somet'ing loose and if we don't take t'e baby, he might not make it."

"We have no anesthetic…" Carl began.

"I don't care!" I cried, grabbing the doctor's hand. "Do it, Gustav. You have to save my baby!"

He looked into my eyes. I stared back and noted his shock as he saw the determination in their depths. I would do whatever it took, endure anything.

"You are a brave woman, Dr. Laralee. T'is will hurt like hell, but t'ere is no ot'er way."

Turning to Carl, he said, "Find a stick as big as your t'umb and clean it quickly. Tell Teresa to boil t'e sharpest knife we have and some fabric."

As soon as he left, Gustav turned to me. "You know I must cut open your belly wit'out anyt'ing to numb t'e pain."

"Yes."

"I may not be able to save you bot'."

"Then save my child. Promise me, Gustav! You will save my baby!"

He nodded. "I will do all t'at I can."

Carl rushed up, wild-eyed and disheveled, and held out the stick. "Will this work?"

"Ya, it is perfect," Gustav said. He looked me in the eyes again and nodded. "Now…it is time."

Teresa brought the knife, as sterilized as it could be, and Gustav ordered everyone outside.

"I'm staying," Carl said, taking my hand.

I gazed into the face of the man I loved more than life itself and knew I must send him away. He could not handle the pain I was about to endure.

"No, you must go, my love. This will not be pleasant, and Gustav and I must do this alone."

"I can help," Teresa said. Taking Carl by the arm, she led him to the door. "Go and wait with the others. I'll call you when it's done. She has to fight for the child's life and cannot be distracted."

I heard voices as the men led Carl away from the house. A contraction took me by surprise and a moan became a scream as the wave of pain accelerated, multiplied tenfold by the new searing agony deep inside.

Teresa helped remove my clothing, using my shirt as a sheet for modesty's sake.

Gustav washed my abdomen with the cloth Teresa had boiled and held the stick up to my face. "T'is is for you to bite on. T'e pain... I cannot do anyt'ing about it. You must endure it for t'e baby. I will be as quick as I can."

Teresa took my hand. "Squeeze as hard as you need to," she said as Gustav turned his attention to my belly.

I made one more moaning comment before the pain began. "Save my baby."

The pocketknife seemed to slice through skin and muscle and tissue at a snail's pace, my every nerve screaming in agony. I screwed my eyes shut, bit down on the stick, and nearly crushed Teresa's hand. Blood flowed freely down my sides. Screams sounded all around me. They echoed in my head and my last coherent thought was, *Damn that noise! Somebody make it stop!*

***

I groaned. Pain enveloped me in a furious assault as though angry I had passed out.

Carl appeared at my side looking like he hadn't slept in weeks. "Laralee, my love…" His voice cracked as he raised my hand to his lips.

"The baby?" I whispered, my mouth and throat dry as sandpaper.

"He's fine—healthy and crying for his mother. He's hungry."

I heaved a sigh of relief as joyful tears filled my eyes. "Gustav saved him."

"He saved you both."

"Water."

Using the cup he'd made from the bottle Angie and I had found, he gave me three sips of cool water that tasted like heaven.

"What did you name him?"

"I couldn't name him without input from his mother. We talked about Martin and Morley—which do you prefer?"

"I have to see him first. He has to fit the name."

Carl laughed. "Of course. Just a minute." He went to the door and waved, returning to sit beside me. His voice soft, he said, "You've been unconscious for a week, Laralee. You lost a lot of blood and the cut got infected. The fall damaged something inside you and Gustav said we can't have more children. Are you okay with just one?"

He had always talked about having a houseful of kids, but that was before we found ourselves stranded on an island in the middle of nowhere. I smiled. "I'm fine with one, Carl. We can spoil him rotten."

I thought about how tired I felt and couldn't imagine having the energy to chase after a half-dozen kids. *Maybe in a few days I'll start to regain my energy. Then again, they say a mother always knows… Perhaps this is all the time I'll have with him.*

Just then, Teresa carried a mewling little bundle in and laid him on my chest. Red-faced from crying, he squinched his eyes shut, opened his mouth wide, and let out a yowl.

"He's hungry," Teresa said, helping me open my top.

As his mouth closed on my nipple, he opened his eyes and gazed into my face. He stopped suckling, stared for a long moment, and made a happy, satisfied chortle as he resumed his meal. My heart nearly burst with the deepest, purest love I had ever experienced. What I had endured to bring him into the world seemed trivial and I knew I would do it a hundred times over to be able to hold him in my arms like this…even just once.

"You are so beautiful," Carl murmured. "My Madonna and child."

I smiled through my tears and said, "Morley. He's a Morley through and through."

PART II

Chapter 13

Twelve years later...

"**THROW IT HERE,** Bob!" I yelled, raising both hands to catch the tossed coconut. The hard-shelled fruit sailed high over Andy's outstretched arms and settled softly into my hand. I ran to the finish line on the sandy beach, raised the coconut into the air and did a little hip-shaking, high-stepping victory dance.

"Ah-h, you guys always win," ten-year-old Andy moaned, scuffling his tanned toes in the sand.

Bob ran up and roughly mussed the smaller boy's blond curls. He smirked and said, "We're older, we're bigger, and we're faster than you. You'll grow up—but you'll never *catch* up!" he joked, poking the younger boy hard in the side and then dashing off.

Andy looked up at me with a glimmer of tears in his eyes. "Why is he so mean to me, Morley?"

"He's not trying to be mean," I said, putting my arm around his thin shoulders. "He just has a weird sense of humor. Come on, it's almost dinner time. Let's head back to Town Hall."

Just then, Sheila's voice called, "A-a-a-ndy-y-y-y? It's dinner time!"

"Coming, Mom!"

"How come you don't have a mom or dad, Morley?" Andy asked as we walked along the trail. "It must be great not having anyone telling you what to do all the time."

I felt the familiar sadness settle in my heart and I almost agreed with him just to avoid talking about it. But his earlier tears and feeling of being picked on by Bob made me want to share a bit of my own unhappiness—just so he wouldn't feel so alone.

"Sometimes it's cool not having anyone telling me what to do," I agreed, "but at least you know your parents love you. My dad kind of lost his mind when my mom died—I was only three—and most of the time I don't think he even cared where I was or what I was doing. Everyone in the village helped raise me because I don't have a family. It's kinda lonely."

"Gee, I never thought of it like that. My mom and dad must love me a *lot*—they always ask where I was and what I did!"

We laughed as we walked up to Town Hall.

"Morley, do you want to sit with us tonight?" Sheila asked. She and Guillermo cooked dinner for the village every evening and they usually invited me to join them.

"Sure, thanks."

"You boys go wash up at the creek and head back here. Be careful! The food's about ready."

Andy seemed fascinated by my revelation. "So, how'd your parents die?"

"Mom had a really hard time when I was born. Something was wrong, and I guess Doc Gustav had to cut her open to get me out. She lost a lot of blood. Then the cut got infected. She almost died and never did get real strong again."

I looked down at the ground and told him something I'd never told anyone else. Ever.

"I think my dad blamed me," I murmured. "I don't know how many times he told me he loved her more than life itself. I think he wished I died instead of my mom."

Evidently, Andy couldn't think of anything else to say to that because he quit asking questions. And he never brought it up again.

The sadness had taken root and I was quiet throughout dinner. Didn't eat much. I excused myself and said I was going home but went into the jungle instead where I could cry, and no one would see. Andy's questions had stirred up feelings I always tried to disregard, but tonight they wouldn't be ignored. I remembered how my mom held me in her arms, the way she smelled when I nestled my face into her neck, how soft her long, blonde hair felt as it brushed my cheek. But as hard as I tried, I couldn't recall her face. *What kind of a son couldn't remember what his own mother looked like?*

It was quiet here and the foliage muffled my sobs, the tall trees making me feel safe, although I was alert to any sounds from the canopy. Over the years, the monkeys had become more vigilant, bolder, and I knew I shouldn't be in the forest alone but yearned for the peaceful solitude.

Finally, I dried my tears. Many times, over the years, the jungle had welcomed me and helped ease my guilt, pain, and sadness, sharing and lessening my deepest loss.

As the tear tracks dried upon my cheeks, I gazed at the muted light filtering through the trees. The rich soil underfoot produced a moist, earthy scent and the crickets began their evening serenade.

The birds sang a lot during the day but went quiet at night. A few of them—Doc Gustav called them nocturnal—hunted after dark, but most slept and woke up at sunrise.

In the past, if I sat real quiet and still sometimes rabbits and squirrels would take food from my hand and once, a jungle cat leapt over me to climb the tree I was sitting against. Its soft, bushy tail brushed across my face when it sailed by and I sat and watched it wash itself on a branch above me. He snarled in surprise when I got up to walk away—I don't think he realized I was there. Now, there were a lot fewer small animals in the forest.

Growing up, sometimes I spent the whole night in the jungle, feeling more at home there than in the house I'd shared with my parents so long ago. I'd build a nest in the trees and sleep in the crook of several branches. Even when I was little, my dad never came looking for me when I didn't go home. I think his heart broke when Mom died and all the love he once felt for me dribbled out of the cracks.

I was only eight when Doc Gustav found my dad dead on his bed of palm fronds. Maybe he lied to me, so I wouldn't feel like it was my fault, but he said he couldn't find a cause of death—Dad just went to sleep and didn't wake up. Sometimes I still wonder about that. My dad loved my mom so much that he died to be with her instead of living to be with me. A love like that's a wondrous thing except for the guilt it heaps on those left behind.

By the next morning, the mantle of sadness had lifted and Bob, Andy, and I hiked up the mountain. Vicente and Angie and Guillermo and Sheila were lenient with Bob and Andy, allowing them to do pretty much whatever they wanted, except for swimming in the ocean. They knew we all stuck together and looked out for each other. But they insisted we take knives and spears with us in case we encountered a monkey.

As we trudged up a steep incline, I recalled the time a group from the village had gone to the beach and Bob had run into the water. He was only five and was so excited to go swimming that he just couldn't wait. Angie had screamed, and

Vicente ran to scoop him up, throwing him over his shoulder and dashing for shore.

A shark fin broke the surface not far from where Vicente had yanked his son out of the water. None of us kids ever ventured into the surf again—even if our parents were nowhere around.

On hot days we'd find a pool in one of the many streams that traversed the jungle and swim and splash and play on the rocks. It cooled us down and we didn't have to watch for sharks.

"Hey, Morley, are you coming or are you gonna stand there and stare at the rocks?" Bob yelled.

I shook my head and hollered back. "I'm coming. Gimme a break." Sometimes Bob got on my nerves, too. He thought he was tougher than me although we were the same age and always tried to take the lead. Usually, I just let him do it, even if I thought he was wrong. It's not like there was anybody else to hang out with—the only other kids in our village were Bob and Andy's younger sisters and who wanted to hang out with *them*?

We made it to the top of the incline and stopped to rest. The view from here was awesome and today's weather was sunny and clear—it seemed we could see forever. We ought to be able to spot some other islands, but, as usual, it was only water, water, and more water.

Leaning against a scrubby tree growing out of the side of the mountain, I gazed up at the peak above. "One of these days, I want to climb up there." I pointed.

"Why?" Andy asked.

"I just want to see what's on the other side. Who knows, maybe there are more people living over there."

Bob snorted derisively. "Yeah, right. Like our parents didn't check it out a long time ago."

"Maybe they did. Maybe they didn't. Doesn't mean *we* can't have a look."

"I'll go with you, Morley," Andy said, eager with excitement. "I'd like to see what's over there."

"Okay," I grinned at the younger boy. "Someday we'll plan a camping trip and go exploring." I scrambled to my feet. "We'd better get back. Your mom will be mad if we're not back by dinner."

We hiked down the mountain, but my mind was already climbing the peak.

My dad hadn't spent much time with me before he died, but Bob and Andy's parents had taken turns doing what they called 'home schooling'. I was included in the group that learned how to speak proper English. They had told us about things called books and pens and paper, but we'd learned how to write by drawing letters in the sand with sticks. I could write my name and was the best speller of all—Bob couldn't beat me at *that!*

Angie used to tell us fantastic stories and said people wrote things like that in books so others could read them. It would be like going on a remarkable adventure without leaving home. You could fight dragons and wolves and sail across the ocean and meet people from far away from the safety of your own house. That sounded amazing, but I thought it would be more exciting to actually *do* those things—and again, I thought about climbing the mountain and finding out what lived on the other side.

As we grew older, Bob terrorized Andy mercilessly and his mean streak widened. The younger boy was smaller built and slim, unable to defend himself against a bully like Bob. I tried to intervene, but he started picking on the boy when I wasn't around, and I often found Andy near tears, bruised and bloody. Bob just laughed when I told him to leave the kid alone.

Andy and I began to spend more time alone together, leaving Bob on his own. We devised a workout schedule and created a series of exercises to build muscle, running up and down mountainous inclines to develop stamina and sure-footedness. Eventually, Andy's physique and confidence improved and he could lift more weight, throw rocks more accurately, and beat me in all our up- and downhill races.

One day about eight months later, Andy and I were hanging out by the creek, tossing pebbles into the water. The lazy, sunny afternoon was made for a dip in the pool and a friendly, waterside chat.

Suddenly, Bob lunged out of the brush and violently shoved Andy into the water. His head narrowly missed a large rock, but his arm slammed into it, hard, and he yelped in pain.

"What's the matter, you sissy? Are you gonna cry?" Bob taunted from the water's edge. "I've missed you guys. There's nobody else to pick on and you cry like a little girl. Wa-a-a, w-a-a-a."

Andy never said a word. He walked slowly to the bank and pulled himself up out of the water.

I decided to let nature take its course. He was ready.

Bob continued laughing at him. "You look like a drowned cat. Here, kitty, kitty."

Advancing slowly, Andy stopped a couple of feet in front of his tormenter, his expression determined and unafraid. "You want to take a swing at me, Bob? Did you come to draw blood?"

The bully couldn't pass up the taunt. He pulled back his right arm for a deadly blow as Andy quickly delivered a stabbing left to his chin. Bob staggered and the younger boy moved in with a right jab to the nose. Blood spurted and Bob fell to his knees.

"Oh, that probably wasn't the blood you intended, was it, Bob?" Andy asked. "Do you wanna try again?" He pushed his chin out—an obvious invitation.

Bob growled angrily and shoved himself to his feet. His pain sent him charging toward Andy like a raging bull at a fluttering red cape.

Seeming to enjoy the exchange, Andy smiled, pivoted on the balls of his feet, and easily sidestepped the attack. As Bob awkwardly tried to whirl, Andy placed his foot on the bigger boy's side and shoved him backwards into the pool.

Spluttering and coughing, the former bully stayed in the water.

"I'm not afraid of you anymore, Bob. Leave me alone," Andy said as we walked away.

Once out of sight, I slapped my friend on the back. "That was awesome, Andy! I don't think you'll have any more trouble with him."

"Thanks, Morley. If it wasn't for you, he'd have beaten me to a pulp…again. I appreciate all the time you took helping me work out and teaching me how to fight."

"You did the hard part. I just showed you how to do it. Let's go home."

Two weeks later, Bob approached Andy and me at the pool again, but this time he held up his hands to show he meant no harm. "I don't want any trouble, guys. I just came to apologize."

Andy and I looked at each other, skeptical.

"I mean it," Bob said. "There's no one else to hang out with and I'm *not* going to babysit the girls. You whipped me fair and square and I want you to know there aren't any hard feelings. Can we be friends again?"

I eyed Andy and shrugged as if to say, "It's up to you."

He stared at Bob. "You have one chance. I promise I'll kick your ass up the mountain and down the other side if you try to bully me again. Clear?"

"Crystal." Bob stuck out his hand and, following a slight pause, Andy shook it.

After that, the three of us became inseparable. Bob was as good as his word and the mean streak seemed to have drained out of him. I never again saw him treat anyone with disrespect.

We hiked, camped, and explored the shoreline in all directions, preferring to avoid the jungle most of the time. It had become almost empty of wildlife and monkey sightings had grown increasingly common. As we grew older and more familiar with the nearby area, I yearned even more to visit the far side of the mountain.

Bob and Andy's parents allowed the boys free rein as they concentrated on raising and educating the younger children. The boys now each had younger brothers and sisters—five siblings in total.

Teresa and Doc Gustav had become our village elders, white-haired and frail. The Doc had taught Angie as much as he could about doctoring and, over the years, had learned much about the plants that grew on the island. Some were good for intestinal upsets, some were good for fighting infection, and others were great at taking the itch and sting out of insect bites. The occasional broken bone had to be dealt with and when it came to delivering babies, he said Angie had good instincts.

Our village had grown to nineteen and, for the most part, except for the increasing fear of the jungle, it was a happy place. Us kids had never known anything other than the island and it's hard to miss something you've never had. Sometimes the adults would reminisce about food, technology, science, and friends and family they'd left behind. I often overheard them discussing the experiments, vicious monkeys, lovable orangutans, and the shipwreck that had landed them here.

I'd seen lots of monkeys high in the canopy overhead and wondered about that experiment and what it had done to the animals.

My main dream consisted of climbing the mountain and discovering what lay beyond. The older I got, the more persistent that itch to explore became.

By the time I'd lived for nineteen years—on my own for most of that—I figured I was ready for The Big Excursion. Andy and Bob and I talked to their parents. They, of course, were steadfastly against it. We were adamant and determined to go. When I said I was going regardless, the parents realized Bob and Andy would go with me, anyway, and they grudgingly began to help us make the journey safely. We promised to return no matter what we found on the other side and they agreed it would be a good idea to know what was there. Their moms packaged leftover fish and tearfully begged us to be careful.

Their dads sharpened extra knives and spears and made us promise to watch each other's back. Guillermo gave Andy one of the glass shards so we could make cooking fires.

Bruce, in the most magnanimous gesture I'd seen him make, handed me his pocketknife. "Here, Morley, you might need this."

"No, you said you've had it since you were in the Boy Scouts." I tried to give it back.

"You take it. It'll be your good luck charm." He refused to accept it, so I tied it securely onto a short stick and tucked it into the vine around my waist.

Caroline hugged each of us in turn and with tears in her eyes said, "Come back safely, boys. This place won't be the same without you."

Waves, more tears, and wishes for good luck sent us off early one morning for the biggest adventure of our young lives.

Chapter 14

FOR THE FIRST four days, we trudged uphill, sleeping in the trees at night and taking turns keeping watch because it seemed that a small band of monkeys had followed us. Then, the jungle became much less dense and we found ourselves above the tree line with only small, scrubby bushes and boulders lining the faint trail. There, it became more difficult to follow the primates' progress. Without trees to sleep in, we found small caves and pulled rocks across the opening to prevent any unwelcome nighttime visitors.

Our first night sleeping in a cave, I awoke in the dark, early morning hours to hear an animal prowling just outside. An awful stench filled the air in our small space and I nearly gagged. The bright moon provided plenty of light and I studied the shape and form of the animal. I thought it was a monkey and when a furry, almost-human hand reached in between the rocks, I was certain.

I nudged Bob's foot and when his eyes opened, I pointed at the hand groping around the entrance. His nose wrinkled in disgust as he sniffed the rank odor.

Always ready to take the initiative, he picked up his knife and waited as the hand slowly felt its way back in his direction. He stabbed quickly and withdrew so as not to lose his blade.

A terrible screech filled the air and the animal yanked its bleeding hand out of the cave. Instead of retreating as Bob surely had expected, though, the monkey began furiously pulling rocks away from the opening.

Oh, no, now we're trapped with a pissed off monkey at the door!

Of course, by now Andy was awake, too, and aware of the threat. We held a knife in each hand and waited.

Suddenly, nothing... No more rocks rolled away from the opening. There was no breathing or growling from the other side. No shrieks of pain and frustration. Just totally unnerving silence.

Why would the monkey give up? He was injured and angry and he had us trapped.

From what I recalled of the discussions I'd overheard, I knew this monkey was one of those stinking, vicious, experimental animals. They were extremely intelligent and crafty. It would be easier to wait for us to come out and attack in the open than to try and get to us in the more easily defendable cave. It knew we were armed and wouldn't hesitate to strike.

Bob leaned forward to look out the opening the monkey had created and I kicked his foot. He gave me a dirty look and I shook my head.

"What?" he whispered.

I slid over next to Bob and Andy and said softly, "This is one of those experimental monkeys my mom and dad worked on. It's smart. If you were the monkey and you wanted what was in here, what would you do?" I could see Bob considering the situation.

"I'd wait until whatever was inside, came outside," he whispered.

"Exactly." I nodded. "It's going to wait, so we need a plan."

I pictured the narrow trail outside the cave. The steep drop-off fell sharply for at least a hundred feet. The wall going up the mountain was rocky with plenty of places for a nimble monkey to hide and wait.

"Here's what I think we should do. Let's pick up the rocks one by one and move them inside as quietly as possible. We might have to use them as weapons, so we don't want to toss them away. When it gets light, we dash outside. I'll go left. Bob, you go right. Andy, you step out and stay in the center. I'm almost certain the monkey's hiding up above in the rocks. When it jumps down, hold your spear point-up and press your body against the wall. Hopefully, it'll land on one of the spears and we can use its own momentum to force it over the side."

No one said anything for a long moment.

"What if you're wrong?" Andy whispered.

"Let's hope I'm not."

We waited until it was starting to get light and we could just barely make out the shapes of the rocks. One by one, we moved them inside until the opening was relatively clear. I didn't want anyone stumbling and accidentally pitching over the side.

With spears in hand, we lined up at the entrance. I looked at my friends. If I was wrong, we could all die today.

I nodded and stepped onto the trail to the left. Close behind me, Bob went right, and Andy stopped in the center. To be sure we had the monkey's attention, I said in a normal voice, "You ready, guys?"

Pebbles rained down on us and I knew my hunch had been correct. A screech split the air as a body sprang from above, right over my head. I held my spear steady and then stabbed forcefully upwards. I felt it enter the beast's body, leaned back against the wall, and pushed my weapon out over the chasm, using the animal's momentum to my advantage. I let go and watched the hairy brown body sail downwards, the sickening thud moments later a sure sign he wouldn't be getting back up.

We stood there in silence until the adrenaline stopped flowing and the fear hit us. Then we sank to our haunches.

"I'm really glad you were right, Morley," Andy said, his voice quavering.

"Yeah. Me, too."

Once our legs would hold us, we hit the trail again, anxious to leave that cave behind. We even skipped breakfast.

Later, we divided the leftovers and saved enough for several sparse meals. When those were gone, we existed on fruit, nuts, and berries—whatever we found along the way. Eager to cross over the peak, we didn't want to waste time hunting and cooking. There would be time for that later.

We enjoyed the small caves where our body heat warmed the space to keep us comfortable in the night. We made sure we rolled a lot of rocks into the opening but after our initial encounter with the monkey at the cave, we didn't see any more. I wasn't sure what that meant. Were they out there watching? Waiting?

After it seemed we'd been climbing upwards forever, we rounded a bend and came to a dead stop. A rocky overhang jutted out over the trail and I saw nothing in the nearly smooth rock face that offered a finger or toehold with which to scale it.

"I don't believe this!" I exclaimed. "After all these days of hiking upward, we now have nowhere to go…except back down."

"There must be a way around this," Bob said, as usual, unwilling to admit defeat.

Andy sighed and sat down in the dust with his back to the wall.

Savage Isle

Bob and I were running our hands over every inch of the rock, trying to find the slightest niche that might allow us to climb up, when Andy let out a strange squeak.

I turned and glanced back at him. "You okay?"

His face had drained of all color and he lifted a trembling arm to point above the jutting rock. I raised my head to see large, dark eyes set in a hairy, orangish-red primate face peeking over the top of the wall. I gasped and Bob also looked up.

"What the—?" he exclaimed, stepping backwards. His quick movement took him to the very edge of the trail and loose pebbles and dirt fell away from under his feet. His arms pinwheeled as he desperately tried to regain his balance.

As he began to fall, an orange blur leaped down from above and grabbed Bob's flailing arm, yanking him back to the safety of the trail.

Expecting an ensuing violent assault, we screamed and pressed our backs against the wall, pulling out knives that would be more effective in these close quarters than spears.

But instead of attacking, the ape—much larger than the vicious monkeys we'd seen previously—stood motionless at the trail's edge. He cocked his head to one side and then, miraculously, bared his square teeth in what could only be called a smile. He looked so comical and non-threatening that I nearly laughed—possibly due to an overdose of adrenaline. Or maybe hysteria, I didn't know.

When the big beast uttered a soft, "Woo-woo," and rocked slowly back and forth, I lowered my knife and allowed my body to relax. Obviously, he wasn't going to attack.

Bob lowered his knife, too, and Andy whispered, "What's it doing?"

"I don't know, but it doesn't look dangerous," I said. Suddenly, I recalled the adults in the village talking about the friendly, helpful orangutans that were another part of the scientific experiments. *Could this be one of those? Maybe it can help us over this outcropping!*

I decided to try something. Pointing to the top of the rock where the ape had first appeared, I enunciated carefully and slowly said, "Can. You. Help. Us. Get. Up. There?"

As I spoke, I turned my head to look up at the rock.

I suddenly felt the ape's arms around me, lifting me off my feet. He made several leaps up the vertical rock and I dangled upside down in space in the process. From that inverted position, I saw the side of the mountain dropping away in a hundred-foot cliff…and nearly threw up. *I was gonna die!*

In no time at all, the animal turned me right side up and set me gently on my feet. But at that point, my knees buckled and he grabbed me again, helping me sink softly to the ground.

Leaving me there, he leaped back down to the trail and wrapped his arms around Bob who screamed like a little girl and promptly fainted. The ape easily carried his limp form up and over the outcropping, settled him next to me, and went back for Andy.

I watched the younger boy back away from the animal, his face pale, his body trembling. Shaking his head, he whimpered, "No-no-no."

The ape seemed to sense Andy's terror, stopped, sank down onto his haunches, and began to hum a tuneless monkey song. He sat like that, humming, for several minutes and then deliberately reached out a hand to the boy, palm up. No threat. No rush.

Andy stared at the almost-human hand, gazed back into the ape's eyes, and whatever he saw there must've reassured him, because he placed his hand in the much larger one. The ape enveloped Andy gently in his arms and, taking his time, carried the boy up to join us.

Once we were safely reunited on the upside of the outcropping and Bob had regained consciousness, the ape smiled again, uttered a firm, "Woo-woo!" that sounded an awful lot like "Goodbye," and dashed away up the trail.

Shocked, dazed, unable to speak, we sat in silence, replaying the incident in our minds. *What the hell was that?*

It was the most amazing thing that had ever happened to me and now that it was over, I wished the ape had stuck around. With a friend like that, we wouldn't have to worry about those vicious little monkeys!

Bob, evidently realizing he had acted in a less than manly, macho way, said, "You will *never* tell anyone that I fainted today, do you hear me?" He looked Andy and me in the eye. "Do you hear me?"

We nodded, but I couldn't help adding, "But when we're alone, you'll never hear the end of it."

He muttered some expletives and forced himself to his feet. "Let's get going."

I kept my eyes open but never caught another glimpse of our hairy friend.

Finally, we reached the summit. The view was inspiring, but after a quick glance, we started down the other side. For the first couple of hours, the muscles in my legs were happy for the change in direction. After that, it was as difficult going down as it had been heading upwards and I would've been happy for a slight incline.

Fruit was scarce at the higher altitude. For two days we found nothing to eat and came across no freshwater springs. Tired, hungry, and thirsty I began to think we'd been reckless to believe we were ready for this.

At the tree line early the next day, I called a halt. "We need food and water. Let's fan out and hunt for whatever we can find. Don't go too far away, though, and be careful."

I stalked into the trees on high alert. Meat would be welcome—we needed the protein. Water was an absolute must.

Birds sang in the trees, small rodents scurried underfoot. Food was plentiful if only we could catch it.

A rabbit darted away and was gone before I could raise my spear as a squirrel chattered angrily from a branch overhead. *Dammit!*

I glanced upwards just as a large, brown blur leapt from another tree and grabbed the vocal little critter in an almost-human hand. The chatter stopped in an abrupt squeal as long fangs sank into the squirrel's neck. Evil radiated from the monkey when, for a split second, our eyes met. His lips rose in a silent snarl, his long fangs dripping blood.

Frozen in place, I stared until the beast melted into the trees and disappeared as though he'd never been. A rank, rotten-meat smell lingered in the air. My knees buckled. I sank to the ground and shivered.

A nearby rustling caught my attention and my heart stopped. *Oh, my God, had it come back?* I stood and raised my spear, ready for battle.

Snorting and squealing accompanied a crackle of fallen leaves. A wild piglet wandered from under a bush and I threw my weapon without thinking. Still unnerved from the encounter with the monkey, adrenalin fueled my aim and I missed by several inches. The little porker scooted away into the brush.

I ran to pick up the spear, suddenly feeling very vulnerable without it. Additional rustling announced another piglet following in his littermate's footsteps and I took a deep breath. Exhaling, I steadied my arm and let the spear fly.

The animal fell. I raised my fist in triumph, but sudden loud snorts and breaking branches sent me running for the nearest tree. Several hundred pounds of angry, large-tusked mama-sow burst from the brush and charged, her nearsighted piggy eyes looking for the threat to her young.

I hugged the branch and remained motionless, hoping she would go away. Snuffling the ground, the sow found her baby's corpse and nudged it as though trying to help it stand. She turned her head at squealing some distance away and gave the inert piglet one last sniff before fading into the trees—she had other young to tend to.

Listening to the sounds of the sow moving off into the jungle, I waited until sure she couldn't suddenly reappear before descending. Carefully looking around to be sure I was alone, I picked up the prize and called to my friends.

Andy answered. "Over here."

I headed toward his voice and found him putting mangoes and papayas in a pile on the ground.

Bob hollered, too. "I found a stream! This way."

Andy and I each grabbed an armful of fruit and ran in his direction. Leaving the piglet and the fruit on the ground, we joined Bob in the stream.

Drinking our fill and washing the sweat and grime from our exhausted bodies, I debated how to tell my friends of my latest encounter.

"What's the matter with you, Morley?" Bob asked. "You don't look very happy considering we just found water *and* food."

"Yeah, this feels great," Andy added, splashing water in my face.

"Cut it out," I snapped. "I just came face-to-face with a snarling monkey with blood dripping from its fangs. Sorry I'm not up for some horsing around." I stood and stalked out of the water, picked up the pig, and headed into the trees.

"Wait! You saw another one?" Andy called.

I ignored him.

"Hey!" Bob yelled.

They splashed out of the stream and followed me, but at least had sense enough to stop chattering.

Locating a clearing, I built a fire ring, put some dry grass and bits of bark under the glass shard, and sat down to wait for the sun to spark a blaze. Bob and Andy collected firewood.

Finally, while we sat, I talked. "Remember your parents and Doc Gustav talking about the experiments they did on the other island?"

"Yeah," Bob said. "Why?"

"Well..." I paused. "...the experiments made the monkeys vicious and made them eat meat instead of fruit and leaves and stuff."

"Why?" Andy looked puzzled.

"They were supposed to be creating an army for the Spanish government. But the 'why' isn't as important now as what we're going to do about it."

Wearing a somber look, Andy darted glances around the clearing. "So those are the monkeys we've been seeing *here*?"

"Yes. I was only about ten feet away from one and saw it nearly bite the head off a squirrel. It snarled at me with blood dripping from its mouth."

Recalling that vivid image, I shuddered. "We're going to have to be careful and stay alert. I hope the monkeys are more interested in the easy prey on this side of the mountain—rabbits, squirrels, and pigs—and will leave us alone, but we can't count on that. Now that we know they're here, we have to be ready."

After a long pause, I said, "And that ape that helped us over the outcropping… I'm pretty sure it was part of the experiment, too. They were supposed to be really smart, friendly, and helpful to humans—he kinda filled the bill."

"Yeah," Andy said. "That was amazing. Too bad you weren't awake to enjoy it, Bob."

The jab hit a nerve. "Oh, shut up!" Bob stalked away and didn't return until we got the fire started.

As the fire sparked into a small blaze, we fed it twigs and, later, the smell of sizzling meat wafted through the jungle. Our stomachs growled and our mouths watered as we tried to be patient. Fruit took the sharp edge off our hunger but could only do so much.

When the meat fell off the bones, we nearly burnt our mouths wolfing our first real meal in many days. It was the best pork *ever*.

How could I have doubted our readiness for this excursion? We were *men*. We would survive.

From there on down the mountain, we found plentiful fruit, nuts, berries, meat, and water. Although we often heard rustling in the foliage and saw monkeys swinging from branch to branch high in the canopy, we had no further encounters. There was easier prey.

In high spirits, we strode along the trail and for the umpteenth time I wondered who or what had made this path.

A mouthwatering aroma assailed my nostrils. I stopped so suddenly the other two ran into my back.

"Wha…?"

I held up my hand and made a sharp signal. Silence!

The scent of cooking meat drifted through the trees. We looked at each other, eyes wide. We were not alone.

As silently as possible, we crept ahead. Voices called to each other and I realized they spoke English and weren't trying to be quiet.

I motioned to the others that I was going to climb a tree to get a better view. They nodded.

Selecting a sturdy one nearby, I shimmied up the trunk. Once I reached the lowermost branches, it was easy going. An unobstructed vista of a good-sized village showed thatched-roof huts on stilts that could've been replicas of ours.

My heart thundered as I watched the only people other than my own family group that I had ever seen.

Several men carrying spears came out of a house and headed toward the beach—from my vantage point, I could see it a short distance away. They must be going fishing.

Women tended to a group of youngsters in the shade of a nearby tree.

A movement in the shadows caught my eye and I turned to see the most exquisite creature that could ever have walked the earth. About my age, she had long, blonde hair that curled a bit at the ends, shining like gold in the bright afternoon sunlight. It framed a pale face slightly hidden in the shade of a battered, large-brimmed hat. An ill-fitting, sleeveless blouse hung from her shoulders to the top of her thighs, the faded red a spot of color in the shadows between the houses. Dark shorts showed off long, shapely, well-muscled legs, and small, rounded breasts bounced slightly as she walked. Carrying a dented metal pail, she strode with purpose.

I swallowed hard, a sudden lump filling my throat. Sweat lined my upper lip and I couldn't tear my gaze from the sight of her. My body reacted in unusual ways and I shifted my weight on the branch.

A memory came sharply into focus. Once, Bob and I had spied on his parents and had seen how a man's body responded to a naked woman—and what they did together. My own experience had been limited to my thoughts and my hands.

The sight of this exquisite creature elicited the same type of uncontrollable reaction and I grew as hard as the branch I clung to.

She noticed the movement in the tree and glanced upwards.

I froze.

She entered the jungle and I wriggled around to gauge her direction. *She's going to the stream.*

I glanced toward Bob and Andy. They had moved farther away and seemed engrossed in the village life playing out before them. Sliding down the tree trunk, I silently followed the girl and hid in a stand of nearby saplings. I watched her fill the pail. Graceful, strong, and beautiful, she had my rapt attention.

Leaving the bucket on the ground, she suddenly whirled to face me, a wickedly sharp, bone knife in her hand. "Who are you and why are you watching me?" she demanded. Her voice contained a fearful quaver even though she appeared more than capable of protecting herself.

Stunned, I retreated a step and stammered, "I…um… How did you know I was here?"

"You weren't exactly quiet. I saw you in the tree earlier." Her eyes darted left to right as though looking for an escape route, then settled on me again. "I know everyone in my village. Who are you? Where did you come from?"

"My name's Morley," I said softly, not wanting her to run away. "I came from the far side of the island…over the mountain."

"Why?" A hint of curiosity mingled with the fear in her voice.

"I'd always wondered what was over here…if there might be more people." I gave a tentative smile, hoping she'd find me harmless. "I was right."

"Why did you want to find more people?"

"I was born on this island and have never seen anyone outside my village. I was curious. Aren't you?"

Slowly, I stepped from behind the trees. Her knife edged upwards a few inches and a panicky look filled her eyes.

I could only imagine what she must think of me. Angie had made my rabbit-skin shirt and pants when she'd stitched some for Bob, but they seemed crude compared to the girl's clothes. I'd pulled my long, dark hair back and tied it with a length of vine, but my beard grew thick and bushy. *Please don't be scared.*

Extending my hands out to the side, palms up, I said, "I'm not going to hurt you. I just want to talk."

"O-kay," she said, still sounding unsure. "You stay over there." She lowered the knife but maintained a tight grip. "So, there's another village on the other side of the mountain?" she asked, moving to stand near a log. "Are there a lot of people?"

"Not a lot. There are…" I stopped to think. "…nineteen. How many are in your group? And how did you end up here?"

As she talked, I sank down onto the ground, crossed my ankles, and wrapped my arms around my knees. I listened intently. Her voice sounded like music.

"Twelve years ago, my parents took my sister and me on a cruise. I was seven and Josie was only four…"

"What's a cruise?" I interrupted. Enthralled with this gorgeous creature, I wanted to understand what she was saying.

She looked at me strangely. "A cruise is a voyage on a huge ship. You visit lots of different ports in different countries and get off to shop and go sightseeing."

"Oh, okay." It still didn't make a lot of sense—ports? Shop? Sightsee?—but I wanted her to keep talking.

"For the first week, we had a great time—shopping, eating all kinds of different food, seeing things we don't have at home." She smiled at the memory and took my breath away. Freckles peppered her nose and her blue eyes matched the color of the sea.

"Why do you want to know these things?" she asked.

"Like I said, I'm curious. I've never been anywhere or talked to people other than those I've known all my life. What happened on your cruise?"

Her smile faded. She hung her head and said, "One night a storm blew us off course. It rained buckets and the wind howled something fierce. Mom and Dad brought Josie and me into their bunk and we huddled together to wait until morning. We all got seasick because the ship rocked and rolled so much. It was late at night when the ship lurched and made this horrible crunching-groaning noise."

She looked up and I saw tears in her eyes. Wiping them away with the back of her hand, she said, "Sirens screamed and water started pouring into our room. Dad took us up onto the main deck. The crew was putting people into life rafts and a man jumped into ours while it was being lowered into the water. There wasn't enough room for everybody, so Dad held Josie on his lap while Mom tried to keep hold of me. Giant waves washed over us, and I knew we were all going to die."

Her voice cracked. She gazed off into the distance and it seemed she had forgotten I was there. When she continued, her voice was soft and sad. "A huge wave knocked Dad over the side and Josie slipped out of his arms. Mom screamed, and the other men managed to pull Dad back into the raft, but I'll never forget the terrified look on Josie's face. She looked right at me as a wave carried her away. I never saw her again."

"I'm sorry about your sister," I said softly.

"It wasn't fair," she murmured. "She was too young."

"No, it wasn't. But…"

A voice cut through the trees. "Catrina! Catrina, where are you?"

"That's me. I have to go."

"Will you meet me here tomorrow?" I asked quickly. "Can we talk again?" I couldn't let her go without knowing I'd see her again.

"Maybe. Alright." She grabbed the pail and ran toward the sound of the voices.

Lost in my thoughts, I stayed on the ground after she left. Eventually, Bob and Andy came looking for me.

"What are you doing, Morley? I thought you were going to climb a tree." Bob's voice intruded on my reverie.

"I did. I met a girl."

"What?" he asked, looking around. "I think you must've fallen out of the tree—you're hallucinating. I don't see any girl."

"She came to get water and we talked. Her name's Catrina and I'm going to see her again tomorrow."

"We saw some guys about our age and we want to meet them," Andy said. "You want to come with us?"

"If we're going to meet these people, I think we should clean up a little. Catrina wore clothes made of something other than animal skins and her hair was shiny and neat. She seemed afraid of me at first.

"What were the men wearing?"

"Um…I don't know. I didn't notice," Bob said.

Andy shook his head and gave Bob a withering glance. "They wore pants and shirts with buttons. I remember my dad had something like that when I was a kid."

"Not animal skins?" I asked.

"No, definitely not skins."

"Alright, I have an idea."

As we made camp for the night, I said, "We should bathe and use the fire-starter glass to trim our beards. I didn't see any men in the village with long facial hair. We could even cut our hair."

"Why should we do that?" Andy asked.

"If we look more like them, they won't be afraid of us. We can't do anything about our rabbit skins, but we ought to be clean and neat. In the morning, we can go downstream with the fire-starter and take turns cutting each other's hair."

I found it hard to fall asleep that night. Blonde hair and blue eyes nudged sleep aside until I finally dozed, dreaming of her trim form and musical voice.

Chapter 15

AFTER DINNER ONE NIGHT, about a week after Morley, Bob, and Andy had left for the other side of the mountain, we sat around the fire outside Town Hall, a melancholy ambiance filling the still night air.

"It's so quiet without the boys," Sheila said. "I miss their rambunctious antics and joking around. The girls are so much calmer."

"I hope they're okay." Angie sighed and reached over to take Vicente's hand, lacing her fingers through his. She shook her head. "We shouldn't have let them go."

"They're very capable young men—all of them," Guillermo said. "And they're old enough to know what they want to do. We couldn't have stopped them."

"Ya," Gustav added wistfully. "T"ey are men wit' minds of t'eir own." He reached over and patted Sheila's hand. "To a mot'er, her boy should always be safe at home. But a man must make his own way. T"ey will come back. You will see."

Next to me, he groaned and arched his back. "I will go to my bed now. Goot night." Pushing himself up off the rock, he waved at the others and shuffled toward our living quarters.

"I'm tired, too," I said after a moment. "I think I'll join him." Stopping between Sheila and Angie, I leaned down to give them each an affectionate hug. "I'm sure the boys are fine. Try not to worry."

***

Hours later, in the deepest, darkest hours of the night, bloodcurdling screams rent the air. Gustav and I bolted upright on our bed of palm fronds, frozen with terror. The sounds had come from next door, from Caroline and Bruce's place.

Gustav forced himself to his feet, unsteady with the sudden movement and having been awakened from a sound sleep, and staggered to the door. I grabbed the knives and a spear we kept by the bed and quickly dashed to his side, slicing through the vines securing the reinforcing boards. I heard others calling out questions.

"Who is it?"

"What's happening?"

"Is everyone all right?"

The screams chilled my blood and filled my heart with dread. What would we find?

I don't want to see.

Gustav pulled the door open, took the spear, and stepped outside.

Screams echoed through the night, seeming to come from all directions as we ran to our neighbors' door. Using the longest knife, Gustav slid the blade into the narrow slit between the edge of the door and the jamb and desperately sawed upward.

I pressed my hands over my ears to try and drown out the horrible sounds from inside. Screams and snarls. Shrieks and thuds. Wet gnawing. Then…silence so sudden I took a step back, expecting the door to fly open.

I knew, knew beyond a shadow of a doubt that our friends must be dead, but we had to go in. Had to see.

I don't want to see.

Four shadowy figures bounded from the side of the building into the trees, monkey laughter drifting on the still, heavy air.

Finally, the knife sliced through the vines. They gave way and the reinforcing boards fell to the floor. Gustav slowly pushed the door inward and I stepped inside, some small part of me hoping to offer help.

The foul odor hit me first. The coppery scent of fresh blood mixed with the rank monkey smell and the feces the animals had thrown at the walls. Stinking streaks marked everything, while a putrid stench rose from steaming brown piles scattered throughout the room. I gagged and clapped a hand over my mouth and nose.

I don't want to see.

My eyes settled on a red mass that I initially thought was a blanket. *Where did they get a blanket?* Then I realized it was Bruce's body, torn and slashed, disemboweled, chewed, and half eaten. Bloody and unrecognizable. One unmarked hand lay about a foot from the palm fronds, totally free of gore, the ragged wrist ending in stringy sinew and a two-inch piece of exposed bone. *How could that be?*

Gustav gently nudged me a bit further inside so he could enter behind me and I took a couple of shaky steps.

I should go check on Caroline. But I don't want to see.

I stepped on something squishy and stopped, afraid of what it might be. Moonlight spilled in through the wide-open door and illuminated the ropy, red intestines coiled under my feet. I turned toward the wall, slipped on the slimy entrails, and vomited, retching repeatedly until my stomach was empty. Then I dry heaved some more.

Finally, weak and trembling, I placed my hand on the wall to shove myself upright and snatched it quickly back, my palm sticky and red.

By then, the rest of the group had crowded into the room but stopped just inside the door, obviously too shocked and overwhelmed to come further. No words, only gasps and sobs.

I swallowed hard, took a few shallow breaths of the foul air, and proceeded through the doorway from Bruce's room to Caroline's. This scene was as bad as the first, if not worse. My friend had been totally torn apart and in the dim moonlight that penetrated this far into the room, I saw an arm here...a leg there...large puddles of blood...and internal organs half-eaten and tossed at the walls. Human-looking handprints dotted the back wall as though the beasts had played and splashed in the blood then made a random print design. A hank of Caroline's hair hung like a tapestry, affixed to the wood by the gore and scalp at the one end.

In shock, my heart breaking, I reached down to caress Caroline's cheek and encountered an eyeball lying beside the poor woman's nose, still attached inside the socket by the optic nerve. I gasped and flinched.

Caroline's clothing had been torn off her torso and I carefully covered what remained of my friend's body, providing her with that last, small amount of dignity.

Taking a few more shallow breaths, I turned and carefully made my way back to the door.

Sheila touched my arm and asked, "Are you okay?"

I stared vacantly and almost imperceptibly shook my head. "Don't go in. You don't want to see."

***

Once we recovered from our initial shock and horror, the men ordered us women to go home and lock our doors. Gustav said, "Vicente, Guillermo, and I will collect t'e bodies and stand guard for the rest of t'e night in case t'e monkeys return."

Drained and nearly in shock, I clung weakly to the side of the house, staggered, and slowly made my way home. Once there, it was like whatever had sustained me left and I broke down, crying inconsolably for my friends.

Gustav found me curled into a ball just before dawn when he returned.

"It was so awful," I sobbed. "They didn't deserve to die like that."

"No, t'ey did not, but t'ere is not'ing we can do for t'em now. Try to sleep. I will come back later."

When daylight had nudged the last of night aside, I regretted the return of the sun and being able to see the true gruesome condition of Bruce and Caroline's hut. The men collected all clothing and body parts and carried everything to the edge of the forest. Taking turns, they dug a hole large enough to accommodate both bodies. I knew Caroline would not want to be alone and figured Bruce wouldn't mind.

Wanting to protect the children from the sight of the grave's grisly contents, Gustav shoved in enough dirt to cover the remains. We decided to finish after our group as a whole had held a funeral for our friends.

Returning to the hut once again, we used fronds and sticks to scrape up the feces and gave the place a cursory cleaning. A lengthy, thorough scrubbing to remove the blood and gore would have to come later.

"Look here," Vicente said, pointing to the ceiling near the back wall in Bruce's portion of the house. "The monkeys got in through the roof."

"Ya," Gustav said, gazing upward. "T'ey pulled t'e t'atching aside and climbed in between t'e roof supports."

Guillermo swore and shook his head vehemently. "Damn those beasts! We'll add more saplings to all the roofs today so this doesn't happen again. I'll *not* see more of my friends die like this."

We returned home and organized a brief funeral. Afterwards, the men filled in the grave and placed a marker made of two crossed sticks atop the mound.

Later, everyone spent the day reinforcing all of the hut roofs, determined that the monkeys would not find easy entrance to another of our dwellings.

Chapter 16

BIRDSONG WOKE ME, and I opened my eyes, smiling. *This is going to be a great day!*

We had fruit and leftover pork for breakfast, set a rabbit snare, and then Bob and Andy and I headed downstream.

"Here, you go first." I motioned for Bob to sit on a boulder at the edge of the creek and wrapped a vine around one end of the glass shard. I didn't want to cut my hand.

"Can I cut your hair so it looks like the men in the village?" I asked.

He shrugged. "I don't care. I don't know why we have to do this, anyway."

"Okay, then, hold still." I sawed gently at a hank of hair. Not much happened so I pressed harder.

"Ow!" He squirmed.

"Oh, hold still. You sound like Andy's little sister."

I knew Bob hated to be compared to a girl. After that, he shut up and sat still. Locks of brown hair fell to the ground and eventually, he looked older, more mature. *Too bad I can't trim his attitude while I'm at it.*

When I started on his beard, though, the complaining resumed. "That hurts! You're pulling too hard. Ouch!"

"Okay, I'll stop right now and you can run around half trimmed." I stepped back and laughed.

Andy pointed and snickered. "You're bushy on one side and neat on the other. The guys in the village will have a good laugh at you!"

"Alright. Finish trimming, but don't pull so hard." He fumed and fussed until I was done.

"Andy?" I motioned for him to take Bob's place on the rock. His hair was almost blond and much finer—and easier to cut. Thankfully, he didn't whine the entire time.

I didn't trust Bob to cut my hair without an attempt at getting even, so I gave the shard to Andy. "I want mine shorter than Bob's."

"Okay."

I admit, it did hurt when he pulled and sawed, but I was *not* going to complain. Hanks of dark hair floated to the ground and when he started on my beard, my eyes watered. *Ouch! But if Catrina likes the new look, it'll be worth it.*

"Wow!" Bob exclaimed. "With all that hair on the ground, it looks like we skinned a large animal."

"We skinned *three* large animals," Andy countered.

We stripped and scrubbed our rabbit skins in the water, then laid them out on the rocks. The sun would dry them in no time. Meanwhile, we washed up in the stream and marveled at the feel of short hair.

Later, trimmed, clean, and dry, I was ready and anxious for my meeting. "Why don't you two go on into the village and see if you can make friends? I'll wait here for Catrina."

"Are you afraid if she meets us, she'll like us better than you?" Bob teased.

"Of course not. I just don't want you two spying on us. Go on. Get out of here!"

They walked toward the village and I went back to the stream where she had come for water the previous day. As I waited, doubts assailed me. *Will she come back? Was she too afraid of me? Maybe she didn't like me at all.*

"Hi." Her soft voice startled me.

I jumped up and she stepped back, surprised at the sudden movement.

"Hi," I said. "I didn't hear you."

"Sorry."

"I didn't know if you'd come."

Her gaze traveled over me from head to toe. A frown marred her pretty features. "You look different."

"Different good or different bad?" *Good, I hope, I hope.*

"Good." She smiled and added, "You cut your hair."

We sat on a log—not close, but at least she didn't seem as fearful as the previous day.

"Yes. This, too." I ran my hand over my chin and she smiled. Again, it took my breath away.

"Did you bring your knife today?" I teased, recalling how she'd brandished it.

"Of course." She pulled it out of a pocket. "Am I going to need it?"

"No. Not with me."

I tried to think of something to say to fill the lengthening silence and squirmed on the log.

"You never said how many people are in your village." Finally, something to talk about.

"Forty-three, I think."

"Wow. That's a lot," I said, considering our nineteen.

"Not really," she said, sounding sad. "There were hundreds onboard the ship."

I couldn't imagine that many people all in one place, especially on a ship.

"It must've been huge...the ship, I mean...to hold that many people. How did it float?"

"Cruise ships are huge. I don't know how they float with all those people and equipment onboard."

"Did your clothes come from the ship?"

She looked down and then glanced at my rabbit skins.

"Yes. To finish the story I was telling you yesterday... Many of the overcrowded life rafts drifted away in the storm, but three of them—including ours—ended up in the same area come morning. The storm had ended and the men paddled the rafts close. We tied them together and floated in open water for three days, but on the morning of the fourth, we woke up to find the current had carried us to a beach. A lot of suitcases must've been caught in the same current because many of them washed up on shore, too. That's how we ended up here—with clothes. Even though they might not be the right size, at least we have something to wear. Did you make yours?"

"My friend's mom made them. They're not as nice as yours," I added shyly.

She smoothed the faded blue top as a pink flush stained her cheeks.

"You said you were born here on the island, didn't you?" she asked.

I nodded.

"How did your family end up here?" She seemed curious.

I related the story I'd heard countless times growing up. "Their ship wrecked on the other side of the island about twenty years ago. On that side, the water's rough even on a calm day and sharks patrol the shoreline all the time—we *never* go into the water. They couldn't recover anything from the ship even though you can see the stern sticking up out of the sea a short distance away. All they had was what they were wearing."

Again, an uncomfortable silence filled the air.

"Where are your friends?" she asked. "You said they're here with you, right?"

"They wanted to go meet some of the guys from your village, so I thought it would be a good idea if they went while we talked. Or they'd be spying on us."

She laughed—a melodious, musical sound. "Yes, that sounds like the boys I know, too."

"I'd like to meet the people in your village. I've never seen anyone outside of my family group. Do you think you could introduce me?"

"Alright. It is exciting to meet someone new. I've known everyone in my village since I was seven years old."

I hope she means it's exciting to meet me!

I grinned and hoped I didn't look as goofy as I felt.

"Yesterday right before you ran off, they called you Catrina. I think you look more like a…would it be okay if I call you Kit?"

A blush tinged her cheeks again. "Okay." She looked away, then back again, and said softly, "I'd like that."

We strolled through the trees in a more comfortable silence, dead leaves and twigs crunching underfoot. The sun seemed brighter, the birds chirpier, and the smell of the jungle more intoxicating. *This is the most exciting day of my life!* I was about to meet new people for the first time ever—and Kit was going to introduce us. It didn't get any better than that.

As we left the trees and walked between the first two houses, I heard voices.

"Morley! Hey, Morley! Over here." I turned and saw Bob and Andy heading my way with a group of four or five guys about our age. They shoved and laughed, jostling each other like we used to do.

As usual, Bob took the lead. "Hey, Morley, this is Joe, Pat, Frank, Harley, and Ron."

Each of the guys grunted or made a noncommittal, "Hey" as his name was mentioned, but when Ron was introduced, he frowned and said, "What are you doing with *him*, Catrina?"

"This is my new friend, Morley. He came from the other side of the island with *your* new friends."

"Yeah, so? That doesn't explain why you're with him. Are you sneaking around behind my back?"

"I'm not sneaking. And you have no say in what I do, Ron."

She turned her back to him and said to me, "Come on."

An arm shot out and grabbed Kit's wrist, yanking her backwards. She nearly lost her footing and let out a pained yelp as Ron twisted her arm.

Instinctively, I jerked a knife from the vine around my waist and pivoted on the balls of my feet, wrapping one arm around Ron's neck. With the blade at his throat, I growled, "Let her go."

No one breathed as time stopped.

"Okay, okay," Ron said, letting go of Kit's wrist and holding his hands up in the air. "You can have her if you want her. She's not worth the effort, anyway."

He marched away, rubbing his throat where the tip of the blade had nicked the skin.

"Thanks, Morley," Kit said quietly. "He's always been a troublemaker and, for some reason, thinks we're a couple. I avoid him whenever I can, and my parents have never liked him. When they hear about this, you'll have earned some major brownie points."

"What are brownie points?" I asked, although it sounded like a good thing.

"It's just an expression. It means you'll have gained status."

"Okay." Still puzzled, I decided to go with the flow. I seemed to have missed out on a lot living in a small village.

"Hey, Morley," Andy hollered, "we're going swimming at the stream if you want to come."

I waved to let him know I heard the invitation, but I planned on spending as much time with Kit as possible. We weren't going to be here long.

She stopped in front of a house that looked like all the others. "This is where I live. I'm going to introduce you to my parents and I'm sure they'll have a million questions. Try to be patient."

Stepping inside, she said, "Mom, Dad, I want you to meet my new friend."

A tall, attractive woman and a rugged, barrel-chested man turned at the sound of their daughter's voice.

"A *new* friend?" her mother asked, sounding surprised.

"Yes, this is Morley and he came here from the other side of the island. There's another village over there."

"Really? We assumed we were alone on the island since we'd never seen another human being in all these years." She gave me the once-over and raised an eyebrow.

What does that mean?

I couldn't tell if she disapproved or not, but her voice was slightly cool as she asked, "Where did you two meet?"

"I ran into him at the creek when I went to get water," Kit said lightly.

She left out the part about it being yesterday and I saw no need to correct her.

"You're going to love this, Mom. Ron got nasty when he saw me with Morley and grabbed my wrist. He almost yanked me off my feet and accused me of sneaking around behind his back."

Her mother sighed, frowned, and shook her head. "Why does he act like that?"

Kit gave me a look.

"In the blink of an eye, Morley whipped out a knife and held it to Ron's throat. When he told him to leave me alone, the coward slunk off like a beaten dog. I don't think I'll have any more trouble with him."

"So, you're a force to be reckoned with, are you?" her father said, his voice deep and imposing. He stuck out his hand and said, "Thank you for standing up for Catrina."

I glanced at his hand and wondered what he wanted. Kit took my wrist and guided my hand into her father's. He grasped it firmly and shook, so I grasped and shook back. It seemed we had bonded. Must be those brownie points Kit had mentioned. They had some odd customs on this side of the mountain.

Her parents did, indeed, have many questions and I found myself repeating much of what I'd already told Kit. They invited me to stay for dinner, but I knew I should get back to Bob and Andy—we needed to check the snare.

Kit walked me to the edge of the jungle.

"Can you meet me again tomorrow?" I asked, my heart in my throat.

"Yes, by the stream."

I nearly pranced all the way back to our campsite. Bob and Andy arrived shortly after I'd cleaned the rabbit caught in the day's snare. I already had a cooking fire blazing.

"Why didn't you come to the creek, Morley?" Andy asked. "Pat and Harley and the guys showed us a great swimming hole."

Bob jabbed him with an elbow. "Did you *see* Kit? Would *you* leave her to go swimming with a bunch of guys?" He looked at me and said, "I don't blame you, Mor. I wouldn't have gone swimming, either."

"And you put that jerk Ron in his place," Andy said. "I bet he won't bother her anymore."

Changing the subject, I brought up something we had yet to discuss. "How long do you want to stay here?"

Bob shrugged.

Andy reminded me of my promise to his parents. "You said we'd check it out and return to our village as soon as possible. Mom and Dad will be worried if we stay too long."

"How about if we stay for several days and then head home?" I asked. "I can always come back later if I want."

"Okay," Andy said. "That sounds fair. We can hang around with Pat, Harley, Joe, and Frank and then take off. I doubt Ron will join the group again—he was pretty embarrassed."

Bob nodded. "Yeah, that's okay with me. And Pat said he'd like to go back with us, if we'll have him. He sounded like you, Morley. He's always wondered what was on the other side of the island."

"Sure," I said. "I know how he feels. He's welcome to come with us as long as he can keep up."

Bob laughed. "He's a fitness nut. He could probably outrun, out-throw, and out-fight you. He'll keep up."

"Okay. Once we decide when we're leaving, tell him to meet us at the creek at daybreak. And to bring weapons and jerky or leftovers with him—whatever he can carry."

The next few days sped by too quickly. One afternoon, Kit and I met by the stream just after lunch and I found she could run like a deer, climb like a monkey, and her laughter sounded like joy itself.

Another day we went back to her village and she introduced me to her friends, Sara and Michelle. I was a bit uncomfortable since I'd never spent much time with girls—I had nothing to talk to them about. I much preferred being alone with Kit.

I loved talking, laughing, and playing with her, but had no idea how she felt. She seemed to like being with me since each day she agreed to meet again. *How do boys and girls, men and women, go from being friends to being…more?*

"My mom wants you to come to dinner tonight," Kit said. "She thinks we're spending too much time alone."

"Do you?"

"Do I what?" she asked.

"Think we spend too much time alone."

"No," she said softly. "I like being with you. You make me feel safe."

My heart pounded so hard I was afraid she'd hear.

Dinner was pleasant, but I got the feeling her parents were trying to tell me something. I caught a disapproving glance from Kit's mother after I told a funny story and then jokingly said to Kit, "No jungle cat would ever take you away from *me*."

"You and your friends are leaving soon, aren't you, Morley?" Her father asked the question with unconcealed hope in his voice.

By the time the meal was over, I was anxious to leave for camp, yet dreading the next day—our last together.

That afternoon, neither of us felt like running and playing. We climbed a tree and watched the animals on the jungle floor, saying little. Eventually, the afternoon sun dropped low in the sky.

"My friends and I leave early tomorrow for the other side of the island," I said, breaking the silence.

"I know," she said sadly. "Will I ever see you again?"

"Yes. I promised Andy's parents we wouldn't stay here long, but I'll come back. I swear I will."

Her large blue eyes glimmered with tears, reminding me of sea pools on an overcast day.

"Don't cry, Kit. I won't be gone long."

As we walked slowly to the edge of the jungle, neither of us seeming to want our time together to end, her hand brushed against mine. A tingle ran from my fingertips to my shoulder. I heard her quick, little gasp and knew she felt it, too. Hoping she wouldn't pull away, I tentatively took her hand and smiled as her fingers threaded through mine.

We stopped at the tree line and when she turned to face me, I again saw the shimmer of tears in her eyes. For a long moment she stared at me, then took my face in her hands. Raising her lips to mine, she kissed me softly, long and slow. *A promise of wondrous things to come? But what?* I cursed my inexperience.

"Come back to me, Morley," she whispered and then ran into her village.

I stood in the deepening shadows, feeling the softness of her warm lips on mine, until she disappeared.

Anxious to be gone so I could return, I joined Bob and Andy at camp. We had snared a rabbit and ate well that night in preparation for days of only fruit and nuts.

We climbed into our tree nests early, wanting to get a good night's sleep before beginning the grueling trek home.

Late in the night, a twig cracked. I came fully awake, searching the ground below for the source. Hazy moonlight filtered through the trees and I immediately spotted Ron and two of his friends slinking through our campsite.

Evidently, he didn't get enough the other day.

I saw Bob and Andy watching, too.

Ron's whiny voice carried on the night air. "It looks like they're gone already. Damn. I was looking forward to kicking some mountain man ass."

As luck would have it, they stopped directly under the tree we'd selected for our nests and it was just too tempting. We dropped from above and knocked the intruders to the ground.

"Well, if it's not Ron and his cowardly crew. Here are the mountain men—kick ass if you have the nerve."

The three scrambled to their feet and squared off. I could tell they were eager for battle, but like all cowards, if their victim was willing or able to fight back, they'd return when they could stack the deck. And this time, I'm sure they suspected they'd bitten off more than they could chew.

Ron pulled a wicked-looking knife from his waistband and took a wild swing. I sidestepped the blade and moved in for a jab to his face. Bone crunched and blood spurted from his nose as I grabbed his arm and easily disarmed him.

The other two watched in silence and when Ron cupped his nose and ran, they were hot on his heels.

Our laughter followed them. *I'm sure I have an enemy for life.*

At sunrise, we finished the last of the meat and met Pat at the creek. I took the lead and established a grueling pace, fueled by the memory of that kiss and my desire to return.

Now more knowledgeable about the challenges of the hike, we had hunted the day before leaving the thick jungle and carried leftovers to eat on the trek over the summit. Our energy level and spirits remained high.

Bob was right—Pat was in good shape and easily kept up. He was friendly and talkative, joking around and fitting in well with the group, but I stayed alert to noises in the canopy and surrounding brush.

Above the tree line with only sparse bushes and boulders lining the right edge of the narrow trail and a solid rock wall to the left, I detected a foul smell drifting through the air. I came to a sudden halt. Andy rear-ended me.

"Mor…"

I held up my hand to silence him. Pointing to my nose, I sniffed.

He, Bob, and Pat did the same and wrinkled their noses in disgust. I mouthed "monkeys" and their eyes widened. Pat looked puzzled.

Pulling out our sharpest knives, we proceeded carefully along the path. A curve up ahead could be hiding several of the ferocious beasts, but we had no other options. With me in the lead and Pat at the rear, I hoped nothing could pick us off one-by-one if we stayed in a close-knit group.

We crept to the bend and I tried to see around it. A tiny pebble bounced down and over us, ping-ponging off the mountainside. I looked up just in time to see a brown blur descending from above.

"Hug the wall!" I shouted, pressing my back against the rock.

A monkey leapt from overhead, landing on the edge of the path directly in front of Andy. Bob and I stabbed at the beast from awkward side angles; Pat was too far away to help. Shoving his knife straight ahead and burying it in the brute's chest, Andy turned his head as the animal's face hovered only inches away from his. It shrieked, mouth open, teeth bared…and then it was gone.

It had wrapped its long fingers around Andy's wrist and tried to withdraw the knife, but the hot blood pouring from around the hilt created a slippery, tenuous grip. When the monkey fell backwards off the trail, Andy nearly tumbled with it, but Bob and I each threw an arm across his chest and the animal continued its fall alone. Andy retched from the smell of the creature's putrid breath in his face, vomiting over the rocks lining the pathway.

As the adrenaline receded, our knees gave out and we sank to our butts on the dusty trail.

Tears filled Andy's eyes as he gazed at his blood-drenched hand. "Oh-my-God, oh-my-God…" he repeated.

For once, Bob had no sharp retort, no witty comeback. He wrapped his arm around Andy's shoulders and let him cry.

The boy had looked Death in the face and deserved to let his feelings out however he needed to.

"What the hell was *that?*" Pat asked. "I've never seen a monkey act like that. And, man, did it stink!"

I explained what I knew of the experiments and the monkeys, throwing in my recent encounters with them. "Your village has never had any problems with them?"

"Not that I know of."

"Maybe they stayed on our side of the mountain since food was plentiful. But now that the smaller prey is getting scarce…" The implication was clear and hung in the air like a scarcely veiled threat.

We sat on the trail until Andy had recovered his composure and apologized for coming undone, and when our legs would again support us, we continued down the mountain. Now knowing what was out there, all three of us kept a knife in hand and stayed alert.

As we approached the huge rock that jutted out over the trail, I wondered how we'd scale it without the help of the red-orange ape. Evidently, Andy wondered the same thing.

"Hey, Morley, how are we going to get over that huge rock?"

"I don't know. I guess we'll have to get creative."

"What huge rock?" Pat asked.

"You'll see soon enough," I said, coming to a stop and pointing.

Pat moved to the front of our queue to study the formidable roadblock.

"Hmpf. I see what you mean. How'd you cross it on the way up?"

"You wouldn't believe it if we told you," Bob said, scowling a warning in my direction.

"Try me," Pat said. "I have a pretty open mind."

"Woo-woo! Woo-woo!" A greeting sounded just behind us and Pat nearly leaped off the cliff.

"What the hell is *that?*" he yelled, pressing his back against the side of the mountain and brandishing his knife.

Andy, Bob, and I laughed at his intense reaction and then introduced the ape. "This is how we scaled the rock on the way up," I said. "We had a little help from our friend."

"He's obviously not one of the vicious monkeys," Pat said, eyeballing the big, powerful animal, "but how do you know he's friendly?" He still sounded skeptical.

"He saved my life," Bob said. "That's proof enough for me." Turning to the ape, he held out his hand. "Will you help us over the rock again?"

Seeming to understand the question, the animal took Bob's proffered hand, pulled him over his shoulder and gripping him with only one strong arm, nimbly clambered down the vertical rock. Bob's hands clenched fistfuls of fur and he made it to the trail without screaming or passing out. Progress!

"Amazing!" Pat said.

"You wanna go next?" I asked.

I saw him swallow hard and although his voice was less than confident, he said, "Sure."

The ape agilely climbed up to retrieve his next passenger and when Pat reached out his hand, the animal tossed him over his shoulder and again disappeared downward. This time, though, a scream pierced the air as Pat viewed the world from an upside-down dangle over the cliff edge.

Andy went next.

I was last. And as before, the ape uttered a friendly, "Woo-woo!" and waved as he scaled the rock and disappeared up the trail.

After a moment of silence, Pat said, "You're right. I wouldn't have believed you."

When at last we filed into our village, we had been gone a total of twenty-one days. Sheila spotted us first.

"They're back! They're back!" she yelled, running to Andy and hugging him like he'd been gone for a year. However, when she saw the blood on his shirt, arms, and hands, I thought she was going to pass out.

"What happened? Oh, my God, what happened? Are you alright?" She ran her hands up and down his arms, searching for the source of the blood.

"I'm okay, Mom. I'm okay. It's not mine."

"What happened? Tell me what happened!"

We explained how we'd run into the monkey on the trail and I could see the concerned expression on everyone's face. For some, it must've been a confirmation of their worst fears—they *knew* what the beasts were capable of.

Then Sheila turned to me—and noticed Pat.

"You promised you'd watch over him and come back soon. Thank you. Thank you for keeping him safe." She kissed me on the cheek and hugged me, as well.

"And who's this?" she asked.

The entire village crowded around to meet Pat and while he was introduced, Guillermo embraced his son and shook hands with Bob and me. "Come, you guys must be hungry."

They served dinner early that night. Everyone wanted to hear about our excursion, why we'd cut our hair, and the other village.

"It's larger than ours," I said, "and very similar in appearance. Their cruise ship was wrecked in a storm, too, about twelve years ago and their life rafts blew up on the beach over there. I'll let Pat tell you about that."

All eyes turned to him and everyone listened intently as he explained how their ship went down and they'd floated for days in the rafts.

When he finished and came up for air, Andy exclaimed, "Morley met a girl!"

I elbowed him in the side.

"Well, you did. And you're going back."

Angie put her hand on Andy's shoulder. "Let him tell his story." She turned to me with a question in her eyes.

"Yes, I'm going back as soon as I rest up. I promised I'd return as soon as possible."

"Can you tell us about her?" Angie prompted. "We'd like to know what type of woman is taking you away from us."

I felt my face flush a deep red but figured I might as well get it over with. "Her name's Catrina, but I call her Kit. She has hair the color of gold and eyes the blue of the sea. When she laughs...it contains all the happiness of the world in it."

"Will you stay there?" Sheila asked, smiling as though she already knew the answer.

"Maybe, I think so."

Changing the subject, I told them about killing the piglet and my narrow escape from the sow. Bob and Andy regaled everyone with their stories of meeting the people in the other village and going to the swimming hole with Pat, Harley, Frank, and Joe.

I rolled my eyes when Andy started talking about Ron. He made me sound like a hero and I wasn't comfortable with that. I had done what needed to be done. Nothing more, nothing less.

Before long, I slipped away to the edge of the jungle to think.

Angie found me there a while later. She settled on a nearby log and before she could voice her reason for coming to find me, I said, "Where are Bruce and Caroline? I noticed they weren't at dinner."

She lowered her eyes and her expression turned sad. "Not long after you boys left, the monkeys attacked their hut during the night."

"No! Were they…? Did they…? What happened?"

"It was late at night when we heard the screaming, but by the time we got the reinforcing boards off our doors and ran to help, it was too late."

"What do you mean 'too late'?"

"We found four sets of footprints. The monkeys had climbed up to the roof and pulled the thatching away to create a hole large enough to climb inside. Bruce and Caroline were asleep on their fronds when they were attacked. They never stood a chance."

Tears filled her eyes and made wet tracks down her cheeks.

"I'll spare you the grisly details, Morley, but by the time we managed to force the door open, the beasts had escaped the same way they got in and Bruce and Caroline were dead."

"Oh, my God." I felt tears fill my eyes, too. Then I had a sudden unwelcome thought. "What if they come back?"

"We've reinforced the roofs of each hut. It would be difficult for a monkey to squeeze in between the added saplings so we feel pretty safe now."

We sat in silence for a moment, each lost in our own thoughts, until she broke the stillness. "I wanted to talk to you in private before you leave us again, Morley.

"Your mother saved my life a long time ago and after that we became pretty close. I'd say she was my best friend. So, I've always looked at you as sort of an adopted son."

A long pause made me wonder if she was going to continue. I glanced up to find her studying me intently.

"The way you talk about Kit reminds me of how your mom talked about your dad. They had a love that few people experience. Opportunities are scarce here on this island and I hope you're lucky enough to find something special with Kit."

I nodded and frowned. "How do I know if I'm in love with her? I've never even *liked* a girl before."

Angie sighed. "Even if someone has a lot of chances to meet people, to date, to have relationships, it's not easy to know when you're in love—especially at a young age. It's all new and you don't have anything to compare it to."

"That's what I mean," I said, leaning forward with my elbows on my thighs. "I never even had a normal, loving family growing up. Mom died young, Dad went crazy, and I pretty much roamed around the jungle. How am I supposed to know what real love is? I do know that I love the way she looks, the way she talks, her laughter, and the way I feel when I'm with her. We only had three days together, but I feel like she's my whole life. I *have* to go back."

Blushing again, I squirmed on the log. "Is that normal? Can love happen that fast?"

She came to sit beside me and put her hand on my arm. "Morley, love can take years to grow and develop. Or, it can happen in the blink of an eye and grow and change over time. There is no 'normal'. Do you know if she feels the same way about you?"

I paused, reluctant to share the most intimate thing I'd ever experienced. "She kissed me and asked me to come back to her." Blushing even more, I added, "And she cried when I left."

"You said the other village is larger than ours. Is Kit the same age as you? Has she had the opportunity to meet other young men? To date? Maybe have relationships?"

"Yes, she's my age. There are a lot of guys in her village and I know that jerk Ron was after her for a while. She sounded like she's had more experience than me. She knows more about clothes, travel, cruises, brownie points…"

"Brownie points?" Angie looked baffled.

"When Ron grabbed Kit's arm and I pulled my knife on him, she said her parents never liked the guy and once they heard about how I'd stood up for her, I'd gain some major brownie points. I didn't know what that meant, but it sounded like a good thing."

She grinned. "Yes, it's a good thing to gain brownie points with your girlfriend's parents."

After another pause, she said, "Since choices are so few here, I think going back to see what can happen with Kit makes a lot of sense. If it doesn't work out, you can always come back here. You know we love you." She gave me a quick hug.

A wave of warmth washed over me. "Thanks, Angie. You're the closest thing to a mother I've had. And I don't even remember what Mom looked like." My eyes filled with tears. "Does that make me an awful son?"

"No, no, of course not," she exclaimed. "You were so young when she died, I'd be surprised if you did remember.

Here, let's fill in some of the blanks so you have a clearer picture, okay?"

"Yeah, I'd like that."

"Your parents made a striking pair—Carl tall and handsome, gangly with brown hair and darker eyes; Laralee, short and curvy with pale skin and blonde hair. She barely came up to his chest. When she worked in the lab, she always pulled her hair back in a ponytail but usually wore it loose and soft when she wasn't working."

"Did my mom sing?" I asked. "I seem to remember her singing to me."

"Yes, she often hummed in the lab and I recall her singing to you. She had a lovely voice.

"You very much resemble your father, but I see your mother in you, too. You have a big heart and treat people with kindness. You were the product of an immense love, Morley. Despite the way your father acted after your mom died, don't ever forget they both loved you very much."

We sat in silence for a while and finally I said, "Thank you. Now I have a more complete picture of my mother and don't feel so guilty for not being able to see her in my mind."

"You're welcome, son. You'd better get some sleep—I bet you're exhausted. If you have any more questions about your parents, come see me before you leave. I'll do my best to answer them for you."

That night I nestled into my bed of palm fronds and closed my eyes. At first, I envisioned the monkeys attacking Bruce and Caroline and shed tears for people I'd known all my life. Then, for the first time in many years, my mom's face came clearly to mind, and I fell asleep feeling guilt-free, wrapped in my mother's loving arms.

Chapter 17

AT DINNER a week later, I announced that I'd be leaving in the morning. Pat said he'd like to go back with me and tell his people about our side of the island. Bob and Andy offered to accompany us to the tree line. I gladly accepted. It would be a long trek and I'd enjoy their companionship and camaraderie for a while longer.

Guillermo and Sheila sent extra food. Vicente and Angie made sure my knives and spears sported super-sharp points, even checking with Pat to see if they could improve upon his. I added a couple more knives and spears, in case we ran into more monkeys. Doc Gustav and Teresa shed tears and wished us well. The entire village turned out to see us off—after all, I'd known these people my entire life.

Waving goodbye, my eyes burned with unshed tears and I wondered if this was the last time I would see them.

The first couple of days, Bob, Andy, Pat, and I joked and laughed. Our last day together we grew silent, solemn, unable to put our feelings into words.

After Andy had put Bob in his place and the bullying had stopped, we three had grown close, like brothers. It was hard to think of leaving them behind permanently.

That next morning, we shook hands like men, hugged like brothers, and waved goodbye. Pat and I started up the trail and I hoped the guys didn't see me stumble when my eyes filled with tears and I couldn't place my feet surely on the path.

From then on, my thoughts raced ahead. To Kit. To my new life. *To love?*

I pushed us—probably too hard—stopping only when we couldn't go any farther. And I was barely surprised when the red-orange ape appeared at the outcropping once again. I had a feeling he'd been watching us, perhaps following to help keep us safe. We'd heard rustling in the trees but had no encounters with the vicious monkeys.

The rations Guillermo and Sheila sent got us over the summit and we never took the time to hunt until we'd reached the tree line on the far side of the mountain.

We carefully snared a rabbit and let two piglets go by, preferring to avoid a run-in with a vengeful sow. We ate, slept well, and made our way down the mountain.

Back in the jungle with food a-plenty we made good time, arriving at the familiar stream near nightfall. I sent Pat on to his family and made him promise not to tell anyone—not even his parents—that I had returned. I wanted to see Kit's honest reaction when she saw me again, unexpectedly, face to face.

I rose early the next morning, walked downstream, stripped, and bathed. Although I'd been hiking for a week, I didn't want to smell like it. I even scrubbed and rinsed my dusty skins.

Knowing what time she came for water, I waited in the trees near the stream. The sight of her sent a wave of warmth over my body, my heart thundered—*can she hear it?*—and moisture filled my eyes. *Will she be as happy to see me?*

I let her fill the dented, metal bucket before stepping out of the thicket. "Kit."

She froze and dropped the bucket.

I waited one...two...three heartbeats before softly repeating her name, this time in a whisper. "Kit."

Slowly, she turned toward the sound of my voice. Tears trickled down her cheeks, forming fat drops at her chin.

"You came back," she breathed, her eyes searching my face.

"I promised I would."

"But I couldn't be sure."

"You *can* be sure, Kit. I will *always* come back to you." I stayed where I was, wanting her to take the final step, to come to me, remembering the first time I had stood in this exact same spot. I recalled the fear in her eyes that day, the knife, her body poised to flee.

Come to me, Kit. Please.

Like an arrow released from a bow, she shot across the clearing and flung herself into my arms. I held her to my heart, knowing she could feel it thudding against her breast.

We sank to the forest floor, lips and tongues, arms and legs, moss and vines all tangled together. I wanted her. Oh, God, I wanted her, but I didn't know what to do. Our mouths devoured each other, hungry for...what?

Her hands slipped under my rabbit skin shirt, soft and warm against my back. But when her nails raked my flesh, I grew hard, so hard against her, I thought I'd split the seams of my pants.

I pulled back and gazed into her eyes, looking for...*guidance? Permission? Some idea of what she wanted me to do?*

Hesitantly, I placed one hand over her breast. Swallowing hard, I kneaded the soft mound, feeling the nipple grow hard in my palm.

She whimpered and I stopped, afraid that I'd hurt her.

"Don't stop, Morley."

"Did I hurt you?"

"No," she sighed. "It's such an exquisite feeling."

Voices from the village intruded on my hazy thoughts. *Here…might not be a good idea.*

"Maybe we should go somewhere more private. What if someone comes to the stream?" I whispered.

"I know a place. Come." We scrambled to our feet and she took my hand. "I found it by accident one day. It's beautiful."

She led me upstream to where the creek forked. Without hesitation, she veered to the left and followed the rippling water through the trees. The forest floor sloped slightly upwards, then more steeply, then sharply, and I heard a not-so-distant roar. Rounding a bend, we stopped at the edge of a large pool ringed with boulders and mature trees. A rushing waterfall dropped at least fifty feet from a cliff up above, the splashing droplets creating a brilliant rainbow in the afternoon sunlight.

"This way."

Again, she led me by the hand, following a faint trail around the pool and up alongside the falls. We turned toward the water and stepped into a cave with a low ceiling barely high enough for us to stand upright. Water poured past the front opening, allowing just enough sunlight to filter in for us to see where to place our feet. It was beautiful, magical, quiet yet not quiet at all with the water rushing past only a few feet away.

"How did you find this place?" I asked.

"I was hiking, following the stream, and chased a lizard. It disappeared around the bend and when I turned the corner, here it was. I come here sometimes when I want to be alone. And now, when I want to be alone…with you."

She came into my arms again and pressed against me, surely aware of my almost-instant arousal.

We found a mossy place near the back of the cave and lay down in the softness. Pulling her close, I covered her breast again and heard her quick intake of breath.

Tangled together, I awkwardly tried to pull her long shirt off over her head but caught her arm in the fabric. When she yanked it free, her elbow hit me in the mouth.

"Ow!"

"Oh, no, are you okay?"

"I think so. Is it bleeding?" I patted my bruised lips.

"I can't tell in the dim light. Maybe a little. I'm sorry."

I paused. "Have you ever done this before?"

"No. Have you?"

"No." After a lengthy silence I added, "It would be nice if one of us knew what to do next."

She giggled nervously. "No instruction manual, huh?"

"No, but I know I love kissing you. Come here." That led to some clothes on, some off, a lot of heavy breathing, and more fumbling.

Eventually, I humiliated myself by ending my part of the action too soon.

We lay in the semi-darkness and listened to the water, the birds, and our thudding hearts. Once things returned to normal, Kit said very diplomatically, "Maybe we should go for a swim."

"Good idea."

Gathering our clothes, we put enough on to be decent and followed the trail back down to the pool. Standing next to a large boulder, Kit said, "Turn your back, Morley."

I did. And heard her clothes rustle and then a splash.

"Okay. Your turn," she called from the water.

She faced the waterfall as I doffed my skins and joined her in the pool. The water was cool but not cold—refreshing.

I found that with Kit in my arms, naked as the day we were born, my part of the action was again raring to go. We swam to a secluded space behind the falls. Without clothes to get in the way, and water to help with balance and weight distribution, things progressed more naturally. At least, I didn't get another elbow in the mouth. We did, however, need more practice.

Later, we dressed, sat in the sun, and combed each other's hair, letting it dry in the afternoon heat.

"Your parents won't be happy that I've come back, will they?"

I couldn't see her face—she sat with her back to me, so I could comb her long hair—but I noticed her shoulders slump a bit.

"It's not that they don't like you. They just worry about me. I've never been serious about anyone before."

My heart lurched with joy at her declaration. "So…you're serious about me?"

She twisted around on the rock and looked me in the eye. "What do *you* think? After what we just did!"

Her righteous indignation made me chuckle.

"Yes, I do think you're serious," I answered and saw the spark of outrage leave her eyes. "I've never felt this way about anyone before, either. I just don't want your parents to dislike me."

She took my hand and wove her fingers through mine. "Let's not jump to conclusions. Maybe it won't be a problem."

***

Several weeks later, Kit arrived at the stream furious. As she paced back and forth, she said, "I can't believe my parents! They want me to spend less time in the jungle and more time with the kids in the village. With Har-ley, in particular." She said his name with disgust.

I recalled meeting him when Bob and Andy were here. He was a mild-mannered, wimpy kind of guy and I made the mistake of chuckling.

"You think this is funny?" she asked, whirling to face me.

"No, not at all," I said, regretting the snicker. "I just recall Harley as being a wimp—you'd chew him up and spit him out inside of five minutes."

Her glare softened and before long we burst into laughter.

"You're right, he is a wimp," she said, coming closer and wrapping her arms around me. "After having a real man, I couldn't look twice at someone like that."

My heart swelled with happiness that she thought of me as a 'real man'. Then I felt a wave of sadness that her parents wanted her to be with someone else.

"What are we going to do?" she murmured.

"Come live with me," I blurted without thinking.

Her eyes flew to mine. "What?"

"Come live with me—in the jungle. I know how to hunt and fish and make fires for cooking. We can build a treehouse and live high off the forest floor."

The sadness in her eyes changed to hope and then joy. "Do you mean it?"

"Of course, I mean it! I love you, Kit, and I want us to be together—all the time."

"I need to talk to my mother first."

I sighed. "She'll talk you out of it."

"No, she won't. I love you, too, Morley, and I'll tell her that. She either accepts you or I'll never go back to visit them. If I make Mama understand, she'll handle my father. That's the way it works."

She stepped close to me and raised her lips to mine. I was putty in her hands… The way it works.

"Okay. When will you talk to your mother?"

"Tomorrow morning. Papa will be going fishing, so we can talk without him hearing. I'll come to you in the early afternoon."

"To stay?"

She nodded firmly. "To stay."

We hiked up past the waterfall and I nearly pulled her into our secret place for some alone time. But Kit had some serious talking to do with her mother and if all went well, we'd have plenty of chances to be together like that later.

After Kit left in the early evening, thoughts whirled in my mind until I felt dizzy. *Should I find a location for our treehouse? Or should I let her pick it out? Would she want to be near her parents or somewhere farther away? That might depend on how things go with her mother. Perhaps I should wait and do nothing until I know what she wants. But I don't want her to think I'm lazy.*

Ultimately, I decided to go hunting in the morning and prepare a nice lunch for us. Regardless of what she might want to do about the location of our home, we'd need to eat.

When Kit stormed into the jungle the next day, I didn't quite know how to react. She was furious.

"My mother is an infuriating woman! She said I'm a stubborn, willful daughter. And I told her I was just like *her!*"

We burst out laughing at the absurdity and I knew my life would never be dull. It was exciting just to look at her.

"Did you tell her you were coming to live with me?"

"Yes, I did. And you were right—she tried to talk me out of it. She said it was dangerous and I told her you're big and strong and very capable of protecting me. She said we wouldn't have anything to eat but fruit and nuts and I told her you're an accomplished hunter and fisherman and we'd eat very well. She said I don't know how to cook—which is true—but I told her you're a very good cook."

When she hung her head, I knew the difficult part was ahead. "And?"

"Then she cried."

She raised her eyes to mine and I saw her pain.

"I'm sorry, Kit. I never wanted to hurt you."

"My mom doesn't want to let me go. She lost Josie to the sea and now I'm leaving—she feels lost."

"What about your father? Will she handle him or will he come looking for us to take you home?"

The spark glinted in her eyes again. "I told Mama she needs to make him understand that I love you. If he comes looking for us, I'll never forgive him. I'll never come back to visit and they really will lose me forever."

"Do you think they'll leave us alone?"

She nodded. "I hated to threaten them like that, but it's the only power I have. They'll leave us alone and after a while I'll go visit to prove they did the right thing; that I can live here but still have a relationship with them."

Knowing Kit was going to stay changed everything. She was no longer my girlfriend—she was my mate. And I determined to make her so happy she'd never want to leave.

The rabbit was juicy and tender and Kit thanked me for my thoughtfulness—and good cooking.

"It was my fallback plan."

"What do you mean?"

"I couldn't figure out whether to select a location for our treehouse or wait and let you do it. So, I decided to go hunting instead."

She laughed—that tinkling, joyous sound that I loved so much. "Very diplomatic."

"What do you think about the location?" I asked. "Near your parents? Or farther away?"

"I think we should find a perfect tree in a perfect location near a perfect stream. And whether it's near or far, it'll be perfect—because we'll be together."

My heart swelled with love for this gorgeous creature willing to leave her parents to live with me in the jungle. *How did I get so lucky?*

We spent the rest of the day nearby and made plans to go exploring in the morning. Kit had never slept in a tree, so I went out of my way to make our first night together very special. I don't know how many times I climbed to the crook of the tree carrying vines to lash branches together, palm fronds to make the bed, and piles of moss for extra softness. She was afraid she'd turn over and fall out of the tree, so I even made side rails to prevent such an accident.

As we snuggled together, she giggled. "This is amazing. I never once thought of sleeping in a tree."

Lying awake in each other's arms, we talked quietly until late into the night. A few nocturnal animals hunted below and Kit watched the stalking, the pouncing, the winning or losing, enthralled. Although I explained that a successful hunt meant food for the young, she cried when something died so others could live. Eventually, we slept.

Morning dawned clear and sunny and I couldn't help but think it was a good omen. After fruit for breakfast, we set off on our search for the perfect treehouse location. Rather than trying to find a tree and then see if the setting was suitable, we opted to locate a stream and scout the area around it.

At midday, we found a lovely little creek and followed it toward the sea. It provided unlimited fresh drinking water and widened into a small-but-deep pool we could use for bathing and recreation. Only a short distance from the ocean, we'd have access to fish and other seafood. Now for the tree.

Kit ran from one to another. "How about this one, Morley?" she asked.

"Not tall enough."

"This one?"

"It doesn't have branches suitable for building a floor."

"This?" She asked, sounding a bit less enthusiastic.

"Well, it has potential."

"Really? Did I find our house tree?" She giggled.

I knew I'd have to make it work. She was so excited I couldn't tell her no.

Knowing it would take a while to build the home I had in mind, I searched the immediate area for another tree that we could sleep in while it was under construction.

Thankfully, that was easy. We built a fire ring and I set a couple of rabbit snares while Kit hunted for fruit trees. This was, indeed, a perfect location with fruit, nuts, and berries nearby. I then built us a comfortable bed.

Kit cemented her position as my partner by her willingness to do whatever needed to be done. I fell in love with her on a whole different level that day when she enthusiastically scraped bark from the trees I dragged home.

Wanting her to be as comfortable as possible, my first project was constructing a latrine. I recalled the one at our village and used it as my prototype. Kit couldn't stop talking about it. Close, but not too close; far enough away, but not too far. I even put a thatched roof over it. After all, just because it might be pouring down rain didn't mean you didn't have to use the loo.

We worked non-stop all afternoon and when the sun began to drop below the tops of the trees, I called a halt. After a quick dip in our swimming hole, I checked the snares and found we would have rabbit for dinner.

Kit had never cooked over an open fire. In fact, Kit had never cooked. Her father had provided the food and her mother had created the meals, so I tried to show her how to prepare the meat.

As a child, Kit and her sister had kept pet rabbits, so she didn't want to gut and clean the animal—it reminded her of her bunny. I explained we could either prepare the rabbit for dinner or go hungry and she saw the wisdom in learning cooking chores.

More interested in understanding how to start the fire, Kit soon mastered the art of setting up the kindling and placing the glass above it to trap and magnify the heat of the sun.

Our days fell into a comfortable routine. Up at dawn with fruit and sometimes leftovers for breakfast, we'd then pour ourselves into working on the house. I began by collecting the thickest downed trees I could find for our floor.

A while back, I had stumbled across the skeleton of a long-dead animal and had collected some of the bones I thought might be useful someday. A shoulder blade secured to a sturdy branch became an axe after I ground the flat side to a sharp edge, and a leg bone with a big, heavy knob on one end was our hammer.

We built a ladder by tying rungs onto long poles with fibrous vines and leaned it against the tree at a long, low angle. This helped immensely in carrying wood, vines, and other supplies upwards.

After we'd collected enough thick flooring logs, I showed Kit how to make a rope by braiding three long vines together. Then we hauled the logs twenty feet up into the tree.

Savage Isle

I tied the rope to the center of a log and climbed into the tree to toss it over a heavy branch. Once back on the ground, I tied another vine to one end and said, "I'm going to pull on this rope and raise the log into the air. I need you to climb the tree and pull on that vine..." I pointed to the second one. "...to guide the log to the space I showed you earlier. The first couple will be tricky, but once I lash those down, you'll have a platform to stand on. Okay?"

"Okay!" She took the end of the vine and climbed into the tree. "Ready!"

I pulled and pulled and slowly the heavy log rose into the air, swinging gently to and fro. When it reached the desired height, I yelled, "Alright, now slowly pull it over to you."

She maneuvered the log into the tree, I tied my rope to a nearby trunk, and climbed up beside her. Using vines, we lashed the log to all convenient branches and then descended back to the forest floor. We repeated the procedure again and again until the platform was the size we wanted.

The next morning, sore from the previous day's exertions, we made a thick mud to fill the chinks in between the floor logs—it dried hard and prevented us from catching our toes in the cracks. Slowly, my vision came to life.

The main floor was large enough to accommodate a double-sized bedstead and after building the wooden sleeping box, I said, "Let's take some skins and go to the beach."

"Are we taking the rest of the day off?" Kit asked.

"Nope. You'll see."

At the beach, we filled the skins with sand and trekked home. I lost count of the number of trips we made back and forth, but finally the box was filled with sand. Covered with palm fronds and moss, it made a very inviting sleeping space.

"I won't mind making the bed," Kit said, giggling. "No sheets and blankets to deal with."

Bob's dad had been very creative with furniture and I had helped him a few times. The experience came in handy when I decided the lounging area should include two rustic chairs, so we wouldn't have to always sit on the floor.

Using the homemade axe, I cut branches to an appropriate length for legs, the back, and the seat. I lashed them together with vines and after assembling one, showed Kit how to make a seat cushion to fit.

"Take three vines and braid them together like this," I said. "Make about forty braids. Then weave another vine over, under, over, under the sections like this until you have a square. Make two of those. Collect moss or soft leaves for padding between the squares and use a thinner vine to stitch them together. Voila! A seat cushion."

"Wow! How'd you learn to do this?"

"When you've lived on a deserted island for as long as I have, you learn to do a lot of things," I retorted. "It's either that, or sit on hard, uncomfortable seats made of branches."

She nodded. "The cushion sounds good. If I get stuck, I'll holler."

Shelves provided a bit of storage and a small table occupied one corner.

I wanted the living area enclosed on all four sides with one section made of two panels we could swing open to provide a fabulous, unbroken view of the sea. Open, we could enjoy the view; closed, we were safe and secure. Kit and I worked for weeks on those, but the end result was fantastic.

"I love it!" Kit exclaimed. "The view is amazing! We can lie in bed and look at the ocean."

"When we're in bed, I don't want to look at anything but you," I said, nuzzling her neck.

"If we get started on this," she murmured, "we won't get any more work done today."

"You're right. Days are for work, nights are for play," I said, waggling my eyebrows suggestively and turning back to the work at hand.

Shutters covered all window openings for safety and could be opened to permit air movement, allowing for a 360-degree view.

We both wanted a second patio floor open on all sides. A peaked, thatched roof would offer protection from rain while giving additional space in which to relax or see what was happening below in the immediate area. I talked Kit into making more cushions for the chairs on that floor, as well.

When the house was complete—except for finishing touches that could be created over time—I shortened the ladder and devised a way to haul it up and attach it at the side of the house. That way, it would be difficult for anyone to climb up while we were sleeping. We could also secure it off the ground whenever we went out for the day, ensuring that all would be as we'd left it upon our return.

Life was perfect. Kit and I lived on fruit, fish, rabbit, an occasional piglet, and love. We investigated the island, hiked up and down the mountain—keeping an eye open for the vicious monkeys—and explored each other's body whenever and wherever we chose. Our constant practice paid off and we eventually became skilled at bringing each other pleasure. I never doubted for a moment that Kit and I were meant to be together. I came to fully understand Angie's comment about my parents having an immense love that very few people experience. I, too, had found my soulmate.

The only snag in our relationship was Kit's connection to her parents. According to her, they wanted her to visit every few days.

"Are you going to see your parents again tomorrow?" I asked over lunch.

"Yes, why don't you come with me?"

"You know they don't want me there. I took their little girl away from them."

She pouted. "You'll never win them over if you don't try."

We'd had this conversation a dozen times before. "How does going to dinner at their house and getting the cold shoulder improve the situation? They hardly speak to me, it's uncomfortable, and you usually end up in tears. Just go, have a nice evening, and come home happy."

"But I want my loved ones to love each other, too," she wailed.

I got up and hugged her. "I know you do, Kit, but if they don't want me there, there's not a lot I can do about it. I'll never try to keep you from seeing them. I'll just plan a hunting or fishing trip while you're gone, and we can have fresh meat when you get home."

"You're not being very helpful."

"What more can I do?" I snapped. "They don't even invite me—it's obvious they'd rather I didn't come with you. And I don't want to end up in an argument with them. It's bad enough that I have to argue with *you* about it."

"Well, maybe I should just go today and then you wouldn't *have* to argue with me!"

She stormed down the ladder and started the lengthy walk through the jungle to her parents'.

"Kit. Kit!"

Ignored, I trudged along behind, unwilling to let her make the trip alone. She had never met a vicious monkey face to face and I needed to protect her whether she wanted me there or not.

"Go away!" she tossed over her shoulder. "I can do this."

"I know you can, but I won't let you go by yourself. It's my job to protect you."

"Oh, now I'm a *job!* That makes me feel just wonderful, Morley."

"That's not what I meant, Kit. You know I love you more than anything, but I can't change how your parents feel about me."

We walked in silence the rest of the way. When we reached the stream, she said, "Since you insist on coming to get me, meet me here in three days. I need some time."

She turned and walked away.

It was the first time since she'd come to live with me that she hadn't kissed me goodbye and told me she loved me. I lumbered home with a heavy heart.

***

Three days later, I arrived at the creek early, anxious to see her. I'd missed her and hoped the time away had made her miss me, too. The house had seemed empty. I was miserable.

"Mor!" Kit threw herself into my arms, nearly knocking us both into the creek. "I missed you," she murmured, kissing my neck.

I crushed her in a hug until she begged for breath.

"The house has been empty without you. My *life* has been empty without you." I held her at arm's length and said, "Please, don't ever leave me like that again."

"I'm sorry. I shouldn't have left in anger."

"And I shouldn't have argued with you. You're my world, Kit, and I'll do everything in my power to make you smile. Always."

Chapter 18

WE'D LIVED together for almost a year when Kit became irritable and nauseous. It was unusual for either of us to be sick, but I thought it was probably the flu and made her soups and broths, hoping it would soon pass.

Cranky and miserable, she finally said, "Mor, why don't you take me to my parent's house? Maybe Mama can nurse me back to health."

"You shouldn't be hiking through the jungle while you're sick. It could make things worse."

"I feel awful now and it's not getting any better. I want to go home."

"You *are* home, Kit. *This* is your home."

"You know what I mean, Mor. I don't want to argue. I don't feel good."

Finally, I gave in. I hated to fight with her. We walked slowly through the trees and I didn't stop at the edge of the forest. I was going to deliver her safely to her parents' door whether they liked it or not.

"Catrina! What's the matter, dear?" Her mother greeted her warmly and closed the door in my face.

She was gone for five days. We hadn't been apart that long since she'd come into the jungle to stay and I didn't know when to go get her. Then one morning, she appeared at our fire ring wearing a beautiful smile. She'd walked home alone to bring me amazing news. We were going to be parents.

I felt torn. On one hand, it was incredible, amazing, and I couldn't wait to be a father. On the other, my mother had nearly died in childbirth and I was terrified of losing my love, my mate, my reason for living. *What if...?*

Kit glowed and bubbled, the nausea a thing of the past. She was a beautiful mother-to-be, if anything, even more gorgeous than before. I tried to be as happy as she was, but occasionally went into the jungle alone to cry, petrified of what the future might bring and too scared to share my feelings with her.

She changed, both physically and emotionally. Her belly grew and she couldn't run or climb as fast as before. She would often burst into tears for no reason and when I asked, would deny anything was wrong.

Finally, about six months into the pregnancy, she startled me with a question. "What would you think if I wanted to move back into my parent's house to have the baby?"

"What?" I exclaimed, shocked at the idea. "Why would you want to do that?"

She hung her head and held her belly with both hands. "I'm scared, Morley. What if something goes wrong?"

I couldn't deny the thought hadn't crossed my mind, too, and had no answer. Here, in the jungle, we'd be on our own and I wouldn't be able to help.

"This is *my* child!" I cried. "You know they wouldn't want me there and once the baby comes, they'll keep you from me."

"No, they wouldn't. My place is here with you. I'm just so scared."

Her sad, frightened voice shook me to the core. I *couldn't* lose her—and my child.

"No! I don't want you to go!"

Her arguments were plausible, but I refused to listen. Finally, I stalked into the jungle, unwilling and too afraid to hear more.

Hours later, I returned and held her. We cried and clung to each other. I knew she was right but couldn't admit it.

Several weeks later, she brought it up again. "Morley, we have to decide what we're going to do about the baby."

"I don't have anything to decide. I want you here."

"What if something goes wrong? Your own mother nearly died having you. How can you be so selfish as to put me and our child at risk?"

The fight got ugly and we both said things we shouldn't have. She left, and I let her walk through the jungle alone, heavy with child. My child. I hated myself for it and cried and ranted and threw things, screaming my pain into the trees. For the first time, I understood my father's insanity at my mother's death.

That day on my way home, a monkey had the misfortune to cross my path. It leaped from a tree, snarled viciously only about a foot away, and died instantly when I jumped forward and buried my knife in its chest.

Later, I reflected on my actions and blamed my misery and insane anger for the attack, but it probably saved my life. Had I waited for the animal to attack me I might not have fared so well. And I hated myself even more for allowing Kit to walk home alone, unprotected. *Never again!*

Living alone in our treehouse was the most miserable time of my life. Everywhere I looked, I saw her smile, heard her joyful laughter, felt her touch and loving passion. Logically, I knew it was best for Kit to be with her mother during the birth—I would be less than helpful, no matter how well it went. But emotionally, I was a mess.

I waited a month and couldn't stand it any longer. I had to see her. When I appeared at the door, Kit's father prevented me from entering.

"Go away and don't come back," he said, trying to shut the door.

I put my foot in the opening. "I just want to see Kit…Catrina…and talk to her. Please."

"No. It's not good for her or the baby to be upset."

I tried to see around him and could hear Kit crying in the other room. "I'm not going to upset her. I love her. I just want to talk to her."

He shoved me backwards, away from the house. His eyes narrowed to tiny slits and his hands balled into fists. Leaning toward me, his voice lowered to a steely growl.

"If you come back, if you try to see her, I will kill you. You took her away from us once and caused enough pain already. We lost her sister to the sea—we won't lose her, too." He turned his back and walked away, leaving me outside, helpless and heartbroken.

I returned to our treehouse and counted down the days, guessing when our child might be born. I quit eating, lost weight, and cried myself to sleep.

About a month after her father had threatened me, I awoke suddenly in the wee hours of the morning and I knew. Our child had come. It was a feeling, a knowing, a certainty that couldn't be denied.

After the sun had risen, I went to the creek and bathed, scrubbed the filthy clothes that I had ignored for so long, and ate a mango. Picking nuts and berries along the way, I hiked to the village and hid in the trees, picking a vantage point where I could see into an open window at Kit's house. I waited.

People came and went—they must have heard about the new baby in their midst. Finally, several men came to the door and Kit's father left with them, fishing spear in hand. It was time.

Once the men were out of sight, I went to the door and knocked softly. Kit's mother appeared, a welcoming smile on her face until she saw who it was.

"You must go."

"No! It is *my* child and you cannot keep Kit and the baby from me."

"Mama!" Kit cried from the other room. "Please let him in. You can't send him away without letting him see his child—our child."

The woman's face softened and she lowered her eyes. "You made her happy and gave us a grandchild. You can go in for a moment," she said. "But you *cannot* stay. If he comes back and finds you here…"

I rushed to Kit's side. The baby lay on her chest, asleep, wrapped in his mother's loving arms. He was perfect and beautiful. My child.

Kit smiled. "It's a boy, Morley. I named him Alex."

"Alex," I whispered, beaming at her through my tears. "He's beautiful, Kit." Taking her hand, I tore my eyes from my son. "Are you alright? Was it difficult?"

"Mama says it was no more difficult than any birth. I would do it a thousand times over to be able to hold him like this. He's the most precious thing I've ever seen."

Together, we gazed at our son.

"Would you like to hold him?"

Shocked that she would ask, my voice escaped me. I nodded.

Slowly, she slid her hands under him and held him out to me. "Here, like this. Put one hand under his head for support."

I took him gently and held him to my chest. His scent was like nothing I'd ever smelled before. Pressing my lips to his forehead, I murmured, "Alex, my son."

Something inside me shifted, the world moved on its axis, and I knew I would gladly give my life for this little bundle in my arms. I was his, he was mine, forever and ever. Nothing and no one would ever change that. Love filled my heart, spilled over and permeated my entire being, changing me into a man with a son—into a father.

I looked at Kit and saw tears of pride and happiness shimmering in her eyes. It was the single most perfect moment of my life.

Kit's mother bustled into the room and reached for Alex. I turned away, putting my body between her and my son, holding him close.

"Give him to me," she demanded. "You must go."

"I can't."

"You must."

Kit held her arms out. "Please, Morley. Give him to me."

Tenderly, I placed Alex in her arms and leaned down to kiss him one more time. His skin was so soft and smelled so sweet.

"Now go," her mother demanded. "And don't come back."

I looked at Kit and she shook her head.

I left. I had to think.

Back in the treehouse, I sat in a chair and marveled at the wondrous new being I had helped create. Alex. It was a strong, beautiful name for a precious child—for *my* child. I knew I couldn't stay away regardless of what Kit's father said.

From then on, every other day I would hike to the village and watch from afar. When Kit had recovered from the birth, she took Alex outside and carried him with her through the village. I watched her feeding him at her breast and ached to hold him again.

One morning, I saw her father head to the sea with a fishing spear in hand. Shortly after that, her mother went to another house. From the warm welcome she received, I assumed it was a friendly visit and she'd be gone for a while.

I crept to the window and saw my love nursing our son, alone in the house. "Kit," I whispered.

Startled, she glanced up. "Morley. What are you doing here?"

"I come often to watch you with Alex. He's my son, too. I know your parents are both out and I want to talk to you. Please, can I hold him?"

She brought Alex to the window and handed him to me. This time, the boy was awake and gazed at me with blue eyes like his mother's.

"He's so beautiful."

"Yes, he is. He's the most wonderful gift you could've given me, Morley, and I'll always love you for it."

"Then come home, Kit. Come back with Alex. We can live as a family in our treehouse." Excited, I chattered until I realized she was no longer listening.

Shaking her head, she said, "I can't."

"Why not? Kit, you said yourself you love me. I love you and Alex more than anything on earth and would die protecting you, you know that."

"Yes, I do. And that's exactly why we can't come live with you. In the jungle, it would be only us and if anything happened to you, what would I do? How could I protect him?

"Here, Alex has grandparents who love him, an entire village to help look after him, and other children to play with when he gets older. It's not about you, or me, Morley. It's what's best for Alex. He needs to learn how to communicate and socialize and he can only do that if he lives among people."

Her arguments were valid, but I wanted her to come home. Again, we fought. Bursting into tears, she said, "Leave! Now! And don't come back, Morley. If you do, I'll tell my father."

Turning her back, she took Alex and went to another room where I couldn't see them.

Despondent, I made my way home. As much as I hated to admit it, Kit was right. It would be best for Alex to live in the village, to grow up with other children. I recalled the time I'd spent with Bob and Andy and knew I would've been lonely and miserable without them. I couldn't deprive Alex of the joys of friendship and camaraderie with children his own age because I was selfish and wanted him near.

But just because I couldn't be part of his life didn't mean he couldn't be part of mine. I determined to watch over him, protect him the best I could from a distance—and Kit's father would never have to know.

My days revolved around my son. I'd get up as the sun rose, bathe, have some fruit, perhaps set a rabbit snare, and then hike to the village. Sometimes I'd climb the tree where I had first seen Kit, sometimes I'd hide in the bushes, but my reward was watching my son grow and change before my eyes.

Kit would take him out into the sunshine beside the house and I saw him push himself to his knees and crawl; I watched as he took his very first steps; I heard him say, "Mama", feeling a sharp pang when I realized I'd never hear "Papa" from his lips.

Once, when he was still very young, Kit had placed him on a pile of soft palm fronds for a nap in the shade. Everyone had moved away, talking, collecting fruit, doing normal everyday chores. Only I kept a close eye on Alex.

A movement from the brush caught my eye. A large constrictor slithered toward the precious bundle. Knowing it would only take a minute for the beast to crush the life from my son, I grabbed a sturdy stick and beat the snake to death. Leaving it lying dead in the dirt, I darted back to the jungle.

Several people had heard the commotion and Kit came running. She saw the dead snake and scooped Alex into her arms, crooning to him with tears on her face. When no one was near, she looked into the trees—seemingly right at me—and whispered, "Thank you, Mor." I knew she knew and I was grateful.

For years, I watched over Alex and believed that Kit purposely took him to the same places day after day, knowing I was there. She may have been too afraid to raise him with me in the jungle, but if her parents had been willing, I know she would've welcomed me into our son's life.

Consumed with protecting Kit and Alex, I hadn't noticed that the snares I set eventually yielded far fewer rabbits. The realization snuck up on me. The jungle had grown quiet. Squirrels no longer chattered from above, birds had quit singing in the trees, and I heard little rustling from rodents on the forest floor.

It had been quite a while since I'd heard rooting and squealing from wild pigs or seen the blur of a jungle cat stalking and pouncing on its prey. The only thing I saw more of was the screeching monkeys in the canopy.

The monkeys!

A sudden chill raced up my spine and I had a horrible thought. If the monkeys had moved to this side of the mountain, it must mean the other side no longer contained sufficient prey. *I need to check on the village on the far side of the island to be sure my friends are safe.*

Chapter 19

AFTER MORLEY LEFT to go back to Kit, life in the village resumed a normal routine, but I missed him more than anyone else. Although we weren't blood brothers, Morley had protected me from Bob's bullying and taught me stuff that an older brother would. His leaving left a huge hole in my life and in my heart.

One day while my mother and I enjoyed a rare moment alone, she brought up a touchy subject.

"You miss Morley a lot, don't you, Andy?"

"Yeah, I do. He's like the older brother I never had."

"What about Bob? You two spend a lot of time together."

I snorted.

"What's that mean?" she asked, obviously surprised at my reaction.

"Bob's not the kind of guy I'd choose for a friend if I had any other options."

"But you've been friends for years! I thought you two were close. Am I mistaken?"

"I never said anything because I didn't want you to worry, but when we were younger, Bob bullied me."

"What do you mean 'bullied'?" she asked, putting down the potato she'd been cutting up for dinner.

"He hit me, pushed me around, drew blood, left bruises…you know what bullying means."

"Oh, Andy! You should've said something to your father and me."

"Why, Mom? It would only have made it worse. Besides, Morley took care of it."

"How? How'd he take care of it?" Her voice had become a bit threatening—a Mama looking out for her young.

"Calm down, Mom. We worked out together and he showed me how to defend myself. Remember when you said I was filling out?"

"Yes."

"That was because Morley and I were running up and down the mountain, lifting and throwing heavy rocks, and practicing how to fight."

"And did all this work pay off?"

"In spades! One day Bob came to the swimming hole when Morley and I were there and he shoved me into the pool. I knew the time had come—and I wasn't scared of him anymore! When he came at me, I jabbed him in the nose and hit him alongside the head. Then when he charged me, I pivoted just like Morley had taught me and shoved him into the pool with my foot. It was awesome!" I assumed a fighting stance and threw a few jabs, showing her how I'd fought him.

"And how did Bob react to that?" she asked.

"Morley and I left him bleeding in the pool and two weeks later, he came back to apologize. I didn't know whether to believe him or not, but Morley said it was up to me. I told Bob if he ever bullied me again, I'd kick his ass... Sorry, Mom. ...up the mountain and down the other side. I never had any more trouble with him after that. But he's still not my first choice in friends. I miss Morley."

She wrapped her arms around me in a big hug like she used to do when I was a little kid. Although it felt strange—

after all, I was now a full-grown man—it also felt right. She'd always be my mom.

"I'm proud of you for standing up for yourself, Andy, but I wish you'd told me what was going on with Bob." Then after a moment of silence, she added softly, "I'm glad Morley was there to help you. I miss him, too."

I pulled out of her embrace and turned away to swipe at the tears that had started down my cheeks, suddenly uncomfortable with the closeness. To cover it up, I said, "I'll go get another bucket of water for you. Be back in a minute." I grabbed the pail and walked slowly toward the creek, my mind still on Morley, wondering what my friend was up to and if he'd found what he wanted with Kit. *I wish he'd come back for a visit.*

A high-pitched, terror-filled scream suddenly rent the peaceful afternoon silence, jerking me back into the here and now. The awful sound cut off abruptly in mid-shriek. Chills ran down my spine as I dropped the bucket and sprinted toward the clearing in front of Town Hall. In my fear and haste, I forgot about the large tree root that snaked across the trail and my left toe caught beneath it, sending me plunging headlong to the ground. My forehead slammed into a fallen log and the last sound I heard before everything went black was my mother screaming my name.

***

I had no idea how long I'd been unconscious, but when I slowly opened my eyes, the forest was totally silent. No birds sang. No wind rustled the leaves. No small rodents scurried around under the debris on the jungle floor. And most ominous of all, I heard no voices from the nearby clearing.

I carefully reached up to touch the huge goose egg on my forehead and winced. My fingers came away sticky with blood.

Slowly pushing myself to my feet, I swayed slightly and caught a nearby branch to find my balance and when certain that my legs would hold me up, I made my way along the path. I quietly placed my feet on soft ground, avoiding sticks and twigs that would give away my presence, and listened intently for any signs of life.

At the edge of the forest, I stopped, shocked, horrified. *Mom! No! Mom!* I ran to her body lying in the center of the clearing beside the large rock where she'd been slicing potatoes. *She can't be… We were just talking… How can she be…?* Her head lay at an unnatural angle. *And there's so much blood…* A gaping wound in her throat… *How had it pooled like this?* Wide open, unseeing eyes… *Had she begged for help that didn't come? Where was I? Where was I when she needed me the most?* I was suddenly glad that Morley had left when he had—he, at least as far as I knew, was still alive. I gently closed her eyes, slumped to the ground, and sobbed. *I'm so sorry, Mom! I should've been here with you. I don't know if I could've done anything, but you shouldn't have had to face those awful animals alone. I'm so sorry.*

When I was able to tear my eyes away, I noticed other bodies sprawled around the clearing. Vicente and Angie lay side-by-side, bloodied and torn. *After all they've been through…how could this happen?* Gustav lay across Teresa's body as though trying to protect her even in death. *Oh, Gustav.* My knees shaking, I rose and lurched over to stare down at them. *He loved her so much.*

Forcing my feet forward, I staggered toward Town Hall. *Had anyone survived the massacre? Dad? Bob? Sheila? The girls?* I found the rest of the bodies inside and sank to the ground again, dizzy and sick. *Why? Why hadn't I been here?*

Savage Isle

The monkey-prints everywhere told what had happened. *Those damned vicious bastards!* Trembling, shaking with fury and shock and remorse, I twisted away and vomited into the dirt.

As I slowly got up, I spotted Bob's body lying face-down at the edge of the brush, weapon in hand. Never a quitter, it was obvious he'd been attacked from behind as he was about to throw his spear. He'd died trying to defend the people he cared about. Overcome with guilt at what I'd so recently told my mother, I went to sit with him. Sobs racked my body and I couldn't stop the tears. "I'm sorry I said you weren't a good friend, Bob. You were. You just didn't know how to show it."

When my tears stopped, I stared at the carnage and knew I had some heartbreaking work ahead. I trudged into Town Hall to find digging tools and as my hand closed on a wood-and-stone shovel, I heard shrieks and monkey-chatter outside. My broken heart turned to stone and, leaving the tool, I grasped a knife in one hand and a spear in the other. Soundlessly, I darted to the side of the entryway.

Peering around the edge of the doorway, I saw several beasts dragging my friends' bodies through the dirt, probably to take them back to their lair to feed. *No way. You're not taking my friends anywhere!*

When a particularly brazen brute approached my mother's body, something inside me snapped. I stepped into the doorway, cursed the beast in a primal scream, and flung the spear straight and true, penetrating the animal's chest. It died before it hit the dirt. *Now it's your blood, you evil beast!*

The other monkeys seemed shocked at my bravado and for one brief moment, they froze. Then, shrieking and snarling, one ugly beast scampered toward me on all fours.

I braced myself, remembered Morley's training, and pivoted at the last second, slashing at the animal's neck. Luckily, it had twisted toward me, baring its neck in the process, and the blade sliced a major artery. "Go to hell with the other one!" I shouted, reveling in the hot, red spray that showered over me.

Turning toward the other beasts, I bared my teeth in a snarl, and advanced on them. They held their ground, but after watching two of their own die at my hands, they gave me the respect I had earned and slowly circled at a distance. Fearless, covered in blood, I growled, "Come and get me, you bastards!"

One darted in and received a gash in his arm. I grinned. He snapped and snarled, backing away.

Another moved in closer and leaped forward, grabbing at my arm. The knife sliced deeply into its hand and he, too, backed off, dripping blood.

The third seemed to think, "Oh, the hell with this" and ran at me, screaming and waving his arms, possibly intending to intimidate—but I was far beyond intimidation. I sunk the knife into his chest all the way to the hilt and stared victoriously into the beast's eyes as the life drained away.

Just then, the one with the bloodied arm jumped at me from the left as the other attacked from the right. Yanking the knife from the still-upright-but-dead monkey's chest, I slashed maniacally, left and right, right and left, drawing blood but being forced back. One animal sank his fangs into my knife arm and the other dragged me to the ground.

My last thought was, "At least I took some of you with me!"

Chapter 20

GRABBING WHAT LEFTOVERS I had from the last rabbit, I tucked spears and knives into a vine tied around my waist and took off at a trot. Unable to maintain that pace, I walked as fast as I could and made good time, hearing monkeys high overhead. I wished I could send a message to my friends to let them know I was coming, but knew I'd see them soon.

As I approached the village, I thought it odd that the trail seemed a bit overgrown and I smelled no smoke from cooking fires, heard no shouts and laughter. Calling out, I rounded the last bend and stopped in horror.

The huts were torn apart, many of them already being reclaimed by the jungle. Seeing no movement anywhere, I investigated the closest shelters. Running from hut to hut, I called out the names I knew so well. Tears filled my eyes and dripped into my dusty footprints.

"Bob! Andy! Angie, Vicente! Sheila, Guillermo! Doc! Teresa!"

My voice gave out and I sank onto a log and sobbed. *Gone! They're all gone!*

A screech sounded from behind me and I leapt to my feet. Whirling, I pulled a knife from my belt just as a monkey sprang at me from the brush. My training with Andy all those years ago saved my life as I pivoted and instinctively slashed.

Hot blood gushed as the beast died snarling in the dirt. I recognized its fetid smell.

Alex! I needed to get back to Kit's village. They were certainly not prepared for an attack and would never suspect that monkeys could be so dangerous. Although I'd explained it to Kit, I was sure she hadn't fully understood the risk or shared the information with her parents, afraid they'd refuse to let her venture into the jungle again.

If I had pushed myself the first trip over the mountain, I nearly killed myself getting back. I never stopped unless I could simply not put one foot in front of the other, sleeping only a few hours at a stretch. I ate on the move, the urgency I felt a compelling force. Again, the red-orange ape helped me up and over the outcropping. I knew it couldn't be a coincidence that he was there again—he must be keeping an eye on me. In record time, I reached the brush at the edge of Kit's village.

Exhausted, I parted the branches to watch Kit and Alex in the clearing. But the village seemed deserted.

My heart sinking and Kit's father the least of my worries, I sprinted toward her house and ran inside. The normally neat house was in disarray, items tossed to the floor or broken, Alex's bed turned upside down. My heart stopped when I saw the dark stains marring the floor and dried upon the walls. Again, I ran from house to house, hoping that some, at least, had made it to safety as a group. But I found no one.

The dirt contained a myriad of monkey-prints overlapping in all directions. It seemed they had descended upon the village en masse and wiped out everything that moved. Kit. Alex. My world destroyed.

I went insane that day. Collecting all the knives, clubs, and other weapons I could find, I prowled the jungle for the next week hunting the murderous beasts. I never slept. At times I collapsed for an hour or two and then resumed my mission.

At first, I think they were surprised at my attacks since with the decline in wildlife on the island, nothing else dared confront them. I found they either travelled singly or congregated in small groups, unless planning a concerted attack. And I do believe they 'planned'.

One day, on my way to check a rabbit snare, I discovered a monkey had robbed me of my dinner. Feasting on the flesh that was rightfully mine, he never heard me approach. Insane with grief and furious that I would go hungry that night, I crept up behind him and drew my knife across his throat. As his blood drenched my arm, I thought, "Up close and personal is so much more satisfying."

The endless love I had felt for Kit and my son had morphed into a hatred so deep, so infinite that I had to act or go completely and permanently mad. I reinstated my workout routine, knowing I would have to be in the best condition of my life if I were to continue stalking and killing.

Totally alone on an island in the middle of nowhere at the age of twenty-five, the love of my life and my son horrifically taken from me, I had nothing else to live for. Nothing but hatred and a flaming, red-hot, burning desire for revenge.

I hunted. I stalked. I killed. And lusted for more.

The beasts seemed to respect my fearlessness and somehow knew that I would not surrender or show a sign of weakness. In face-to-face combat they never recklessly charged me, and I developed a good sense of what they would do next. Losing count of the number of bodies I left in my wake, I lived only to see their blood spilling onto the jungle floor.

For years, I hunted, my body a perfect killing machine. I ate when necessary, slept as needed, and not a moment more.

I could smell when they were near and became better at stalking them than they were at hunting me.

Often, I sniffed them out in the caves they frequented high on the mountain trail and tossed burning branches inside. As they darted out, I stood above and swung at their heads with a heavy club, knocking them off the cliff or rendering them unconscious. Those, I dispatched by slamming a large rock down onto their skulls.

Then one morning I awoke to find the overwhelming desire for revenge had dissipated. I was alone and lonely with no hope of ever having another friend, another love, another child.

I walked to the beach and spent a week there. The monkeys never came closer than the edge of the jungle, so I felt relatively safe.

Watching the water, I noticed the nearly constant shark patrol along the shore. It seemed that the monkeys weren't the only unusually aggressive creatures on this savage isle.

Without hope, filled with despair and an infinite sadness, I considered walking into the water and letting the sharks have at it, but couldn't abide the thought of the teeth and excruciating pain. And I wasn't a quitter.

The decision I made that day haunted me for the rest of my life. I would survive. And although Alex couldn't be here with me, I would be the kind of man he could be proud of.

Looking upwards to Heaven, I fell to my knees and held out my hands in supplication. Aloud, I prayed. "My dear God, I have no idea why I must suffer like this, why You took Kit and Alex from me, but I trust that You know what You're doing. I have no one else. I refuse to take my own life so I'm asking You to end my suffering and loneliness for me. However You wish to do that is fine with me."

Satisfied with my request and more at peace than I'd been in a long time, I glanced again at the blue of the sea and thought of Kit's and Alex's eyes. I turned and walked back into the jungle, leaving behind only barefoot prints in the sand.

***

Buy *STRANDED* now to read the rest of the story.

http://www.amazon.com/dp/B01L3J7DGU

Lost at sea. Surrounded by mystery. Can a determined survivor beat the deadly current?

Lissy couldn't resist diving in the crystal-clear waters of Cozumel, Mexico. But when she and her friends are caught in an unrelenting down-current, she counts herself lucky to be one of five survivors washed ashore on a deserted island. Until the tropical paradise reveals itself to be a wilderness populated by monstrous predators…

Besieged by bloodthirsty sharks in the water and carnivorous primates on land, Lissy and the others struggle against devastating odds. And when jealousy creates an ominous rift inside their group, she fears the terrors lurking in the trees will more easily pick them off one by one.

Can Lissy survive this twisted nightmare and lead her small band of castaways to safety?

STRANDED is a pulse-pounding standalone action thriller. If you like whip-smart heroines, nightmarish puzzles, and vicious creatures, then you'll love Beverley Scherberger's savage page-turner.

Beverley Scherberger

Buy now to learn if Lissy and her group survive the daily life-threatening dangers. You'll never look at monkeys the same way again!

http://www.amazon.com/dp/B01L3J7DGU

AUTHOR'S NOTE

THANK YOU for reading *Savage Isle*. I hope you enjoyed it and will take a moment to leave a review at your favorite retailer. They are crucial to letting others know if you think it would be worth their time and they're extremely important to me. Positive reviews get my books more exposure and keep me inspired to write another one that you're sure to enjoy! I read each and every review and, believe me when I say every single one is truly appreciated.

If you've never left a review before, let this be your first! Simply go to the Amazon page where you can review my book.

In *Savage Isle,* I tell the *what-comes-before* part of this horrifying tale. *STRANDED* tells the rest of the story. Read a thrilling excerpt here.

STRANDED

A white-knuckle adventure above and below the sea

A novel

BEVERLEY SCHERBERGER

Publisher's Cataloging-In-Publication Data
(Prepared by The Donohue Group, Inc.)

Names: Scherberger, Beverley.
Title: Stranded : a white-knuckle adventure above and below the sea : a novel / Beverley Scherberger.
Description: Second edition. | [Sedona, Arizona] : [Beverley Scherberger], [2017]
Identifiers: ISBN 978-0-9990543-0-7 | ISBN 0-9990543-0-9
Subjects: LCSH: Scuba divers--Fiction. | Castaways--Fiction. | Shipwreck survival--Fiction. | Island animals--Fiction. | Man-woman relationships--Fiction. | LCGFT: Thrillers (Fiction) | Action and adventure fiction.
Classification: LCC PS3619.C44 S77 2017 | DDC 813/.6--dc23

Copyright © 2016 by Beverley Scherberger
Second Edition Copyright © 2017 by Beverley Scherberger

All rights reserved. No part of this publication may be reproduced, distributed, or transmitted in any form or by any means including photocopying, recording, or other electronic or mechanical methods without the express written permission of the publisher except for the use of brief quotations in a critical book review.

This is a work of fiction. Names, characters, and incidents are a product of the author's imagination. Locales and public names are sometimes used for atmospheric purposes. Any resemblance to actual people, living or dead, or to businesses, companies, or events is entirely coincidental.

Printed in the United States of America.

STRANDED

EXCERPT:

AS RIGO AND I CRUISED downward, we saw the others descending around us. The group leveled off above the bottom at a depth of sixty feet and it quickly became apparent that Captain Carlos was right about the tricky current. We zoomed along, alert for humongous rocks jutting up from the sea floor. Many were as large as small houses, but thankfully, the visibility was good so we could avoid them by angling left or right. At this depth, the water filtered out color, leaving the scene various shades of blue-grey. Darker shadows hid entrances to caverns and swim-through arches created by overlapping rocks. Boulders of all sizes and shapes dotted the floor; stands of spiky Elkhorn Coral decorated the areas in between. As we zoomed over the seascape, the rocky floor gave way to a coral reef punctuated by massive rock formations.

The reef was, indeed, pristine and beautiful. I saw no broken coral or dead white branches. Everything was healthy with a wide variety of marine life. Many different types of sponges and coral provided homes for a plethora of fish, but we were moving so quickly it was impossible to take photos. Afraid of slamming into a boulder if I took my eyes off the path ahead, I held the pricey camera close to my body.

Then, suddenly, it seemed as though a giant hand pushed me toward the bottom. The monster current drove us helplessly downward and I could see the other divers reacting as I did, instinctively and futilely kicking upward. We plunged ever deeper, the sea floor ahead sloping sharply into the dark blue abyss.

Frantic, I grabbed Rigo's hand and he pulled me to his side, motioning toward a huge boulder jutting into our path some distance ahead. Instead of angling to go around it, we turned in the water to meet it feet first. I prayed the current would hold us against the rock, preventing further descent. We desperately needed time to think, to plan.

We struck the hard surface and I felt the jolt throughout my entire body, but my knees cushioned the blow. Held there by the same huge hand that had previously been shoving us downward, I watched my friends zoom past and disappear from view. Horrified, I knew I might never see them again.

Clinging to the rock, I knew we had to find a way out of the down-current. The compressed air in our tanks would cause nitrogen narcosis beyond a depth of 130 feet. Symptoms such as feelings of euphoria, impaired decision-making, and diminished motor skills could cause us to disregard the danger and make incorrect choices concerning our safety. Continuing to descend would certainly be fatal.

Rigo and I tried to slow our breathing. We didn't want to run low on air and compound our serious situation. After a short time, using hand signals, he motioned that we should swim to our left. In the distance was another rocky upthrust we could use for refuge. I suddenly understood. If we could swim *across* the current, we might be able to get out of the strongest downward flow and ascend to a safer depth.

My gauge showed eighty-five feet. I pantomimed crawling up the rock, relieved to see Rigo nod in comprehension. We hugged the rocky slope and slowly made our way fifteen feet up the boulder like a couple of oddly attired and very awkward mountain climbers. Thankfully, the rock wasn't sharp-edged or covered with coral that would cut through our thin dive gloves and shred the knees of our Lycra wetskins. Rough and slightly porous, the surface contained nooks and niches for finger holds and the rock sloped enough that we had no trouble shimmying upward. Our fins prevented us from using our toes to gain further purchase, but the current helped hold us in place.

When the rock narrowed, we stopped and took each other's hand. Our eyes met and we nodded, simultaneously launching ourselves off, kicking hard to the left. We flew through the water and for a while I thought we were going to soar past the next big boulder, but it suddenly loomed large in front of us. We turned and met it feet-first. My gauge read ninety feet.

We rested briefly, shimmied twenty feet to the uppermost portion, and again hurled ourselves into the current. When we finally thudded into the next large rock, my gauge showed ninety-five feet. I looked at my watch to see how long we'd been in the water and found it had been the longest eighteen minutes of my life. Concerned about our depth and bottom time, I checked the laminated NAUI dive chart I wore clipped to my BC. According to the tables, we needed to begin ascending soon or we could end up with the bends. This, too, could be fatal.

We had no choice but to keep moving. This peak was taller than the others and we crawled up to seventy feet before once more taking flight. I thought the flow seemed less powerful and hoped it wasn't just wishful thinking, but when my feet hit the next rock, the impact was much less forceful. I knew we'd reached the outer edge of the current. Almost afraid to check the time, I said a short prayer before raising my wrist.

We'd been underwater for a total of twenty-two minutes and had yet to begin our ascent. The NAUI tables indicated we must hang at fifteen feet for five minutes to offgas enough nitrogen to surface safely. *Would we have enough air?* I reached for Rigo's gauge—only 150psi. Mine read 200. We would normally finish with no less than 500psi in each tank, leaving enough air for the ascent. The good news was that as we ascended, the air would expand. But we needed to start up immediately.

We crept to the pinnacle and took off at a depth of sixty feet. I felt a distinct difference in the force of the downcurrent and we actually made some slight upward progress. The current lessened more and more as we drifted. No more boulders loomed in front of us and I checked my gauge to find we had ascended to fifty feet. Finally we were heading in the right direction. I pointed upward.

Turning vertical in the water, still holding hands, we worked our way toward the surface. At thirty feet, I checked the time – twenty-five total minutes. I slowed our ascent and held up my wrist. Rigo nodded to indicate he knew we'd have to decompress.

At the appointed depth, we stopped and faced each other. The water seemed choppy and we had difficulty maintaining the fifteen-foot depth but it was imperative that we off-gas nitrogen before surfacing. Anxious to board the boat, I'd even welcome a bout of seasickness right now. I just wanted *out* of the water.

We tried to relax and breathe normally although we'd both used up precious air fighting the current and I knew Rigo's tank would soon be empty. Time seemed to stop as I watched the secondhand creep slowly around the dial. With one full minute remaining, Rigo reached for my octopus—a secondary regulator that can be used to buddy breathe. His tank was empty. Afraid to look and see how much air was in mine, I figured it was irrelevant, anyway. We'd breathe this tank down to nothing and then surface to deal with the consequences.

In short order, we sucked the last bit of air from the tank and kicked slowly upward. As we pulled the regulators out of our mouths and gulped for air, we got another shock. Directly overhead ugly storm clouds hung low and threatening. Wind howled, waves tossed us high in the air and then dunked us in the trough, and rain poured down in sheets. Thunder boomed across the water and lightning flashed repeatedly against the black sky. And the boat was nowhere to be seen.

***

Find out if Lissy and her friends survive the current, the storm, and whatever might be lurking in the deep water below:

http://www.amazon.com/dp/B01L3J7DGU

ABOUT THE AUTHOR

Savage Isle is the prequel to *STRANDED*, Beverley Scherberger's debut novel and her first foray into the world of fiction. She began a lifelong love affair with language in the sixth grade when her English teacher introduced the class to short stories. She has since published upward of two hundred nonfiction articles and holds a BA in communication from Miami University of Ohio.

She is also a freelance editor and over the past several years has helped others accomplish their publishing dreams. Her editing website is: **www.selecteditingservices.com**.

She currently resides in Cotacachi, Ecuador, with her beloved kitty Squeak. She enjoys making jewelry, reading by the fire, and—of course—writing. She welcomes reader contact through her Facebook page:

http://www.facebook.com/beverley.scherberger

Made in United States
Orlando, FL
27 May 2025